Heart of the Omega

Fated Mates of Westwood, Volume 2

Reese Spenser

Published by Happy Endings Publishing, 2023.

This is a work of fiction. Similarities to real people, places, or events are entirely coincidental.

HEART OF THE OMEGA

First edition. November 24, 2023.

Copyright © 2023 Reese Spenser.

ISBN: 979-8223200048

Written by Reese Spenser.

Prologue
Rylie

WHEN MY FATHER, MY clan's alpha, demand that I appear before the Council of Elders, I'm duty bound to do so. As an omega on the verge of my first heat, I must present myself to the unmated males of my clan, all potential alphas.

For generations only the alpha-omega union bred alphas and omegas. When my mother, an omega, died giving birth to me after several miscarriages, the shifter magic of our clan began to slowly diminish without an alpha and omega to lead the clan. Because his omega, my mother, failed to bear him a son, my father's reign as alpha can be challenged by any unmated male clan member that descends from the bloodline of an alpha.

Although my father claims he loved my mother, they weren't fated mates. There hasn't been a true alpha-omega mate bond within the clan for more than a hundred years. That's one reason the Council of Elders are desperate for my heat to begin. The alpha-omega bond insures the shifter magic of our clan continues. The magic that allows us to shift, heel quickly, and age slowly. Without it the clan will begin to age and die as naturally as a human. And that's something the Council of Elders won't abide. They will ensure the existence of the clan's magic at all cost. Even if the cost is me. It doesn't matter that the idea of becoming a breeding vessel to a male I don't know repulses me. Or the fact that all my firsts will be observed under the watchful eyes of the Council. That's not exactly how

I imagined my first kiss, and it's definitely not how I want my first heat to be claimed. Unfortunately, to them I'm just a possession, an omega meant to be used as the elders see fit. I've heard it my entire life, *all that matters is preserving the clan*.

Entering Sheridan Springs town hall behind my father, we make our way to the meeting room where the Council of Elders and the potential alpha challengers have gathered. All eyes turn our way when the heavy wooden double doors creaks open announcing our arrival. However, with my father shielding me I'm spared their scrutiny for a little longer.

"Welcome, alpha Branson," a member of the Council greets.

Peeking my head around my father's massive back, my gaze meets the eyes of the challenger for alpha I fear most, Langdon Whitmore. I force myself to look away when his insidious grin, and the menacing black eyes of his bear turns my stomach.

"Bring the omega forward," a second member of the Council instructs.

Forbidden to speak during the presentation, I bite my tongue in an attempt to quell my need to respond. Unfortunately, forcing my words to die in my throat always leaves a bitter taste in my mouth.

"My daughter's name is Rylie," my father corrects.

"Yet she's an omega." The snarky comment comes from one of the challengers, a voice I don't recognize.

"Which is why she should be honored and respected, not shamed."

Hearing my father defend me reminds me that while he's our clan's alpha he has the power to protect me. It also reminds me that soon he'll have to battle one of these challengers for the right to remain alpha of our clan, and if he loses, my life will be over.

"You're quite right, Branson, your daughter Rylie is the daughter of our clan's current alpha, and she'll undoubtedly be the mate of the next alpha. Rylie is indeed entitled to our respect."

Listening to Langdon Whitmore spew his honey covered lie effortlessly, I nearly gag, holding back my response once again. When has any Whitmore ever shown an ounce of respect to a female, let alone an omega?" Like his father, Beauregard Whitmore, Langdon seeks to add to his harem. Claiming an omega's first heat is just another prize he covets. I tell myself there's no way he'll ever get through the challenger rituals let alone defeat my father.

"Well said, son," Beau Langdon says from his seat among the Council of Elders.

Two female Council members approach my father, and without thinking I take an involuntary step back. Wordlessly my father turns to face me, before giving me a tender kiss on my forehead. I watch him leave the meeting room, and I wonder if I'll ever see him again.

"No need to worry, child, the examination is harmless, and it will only take a few minutes."

The stern voice of Preema Ellis tries to assure me of my safety but fails to mention my father's. I've only heard rumors about what happens during the confirmation of an omega's heat, although it may be harmless, it's definitely invasive.

Preema, a beta, is one of three females on the seven-member Council. Although she appears to be only a few years older than me, she's actually closer to my father's age.

Reluctantly, I take Preema's offered hand, and as she leads me away, I hear Beau's crude remarks.

"I can smell her heat already. She'll be begging for a good fuck soon."

"Ignore him," Denna Miles, the newest female member of the Council and the only omega, says from behind me. "It's our job to keep you safe and hidden from the unmated males of our clan until the claiming ceremony. That lecherous old bear won't get near you."

And what about his son, I thought. Will you keep him away from me as well. As if reading my mind, Denna adds.

"We won't know for three more days if the clan has a new alpha. So try not to imagine the worst. If your father wins the final challenge, the Council of Elders will allow you to choose your mate from the challengers. I know it's not ideal, but it's better than having no choice at all."

Exiting the town hall with Preema and Denna at my side, I wish I could say I feel safe and protected surrounded by them. Especially when the small crowd that greets us outside the town hall consists mostly of males. And to make matters worse, my confidence in the two female elders is further tested when the mid-afternoon breeze carries my scent in the air.

Several male shifters pause to sniff the air before taking hurried steps toward us.

"Get her to the vehicle! Preema shouts, rushing ahead to provide a barrier between me and the shifters affected by my omega pheromones.

Without warning Preema shifts, charging toward a crowd of males racing toward us. For a moment my feet stay planted watching Preema give way to a massive brown bear. But it isn't until Preema's bear releases a powerful ear ringing growl that the advancing males come to a stop.

Urging me into a jeep parked a few feet away, Denna hurries to the driver's side. Once behind the wheel she starts the engine and speeds away, leaving Preema to deal with the trouble my impending heat has caused.

• • • •

DENNA AND I HAVE BEEN at the ceremonial lodge deep in the forest of Sheridan Springs for several hours before Preema finally shows up. Looking put together once again, she arrives in time for dinner.

"What took you so long?" Denna asks.

"I had to make sure I wasn't followed by any of the males affected by Rylie's heat."

"The closer you get to your heat the longer the effects last, and you can be tracked easier," Denna explains.

Nodding my understanding, I offer Preema a bowl of the stew I prepared for dinner while Denna was outside securing the perimeter.

"Thank you," she says, accepting a large bowl of beef stew.

"Did you have to hurt anyone to stop them from following us?" I finally ask.

"No, I didn't. The crowd was easy to manage after your scent began to fade."

The question I've needed an answer to my whole life rush to the front of my mind, and this time I refuse to be the obedient omega without a voice.

"What exactly happens during the confirmation of an omega's heat?"

"I've never witness an omega's confirmation," Denna shares.

"On the eve of the claiming ceremony you'll be given an examination to determine the levels of your heat and fertility."

"What kind of examination?"

"I'm sure your father has told you, although your mother was an omega, she wasn't very fertile. Which is why the Council would like some assurance that you'll be able to give birth to the next generation of alphas and omegas."

"That doesn't answer my question," I point out, losing patience with Preema's evasiveness.

"The examination is very similar to that of a human gynecologist with the intentions of arousing you sexually to determine the levels of your heat and fertility."

"You can't be serious?" I ask dumbfounded.

"I can assure you the Council is very serious," Preema replies.

The loss of my appetite has me rising from the dining table. Rushing to the bedroom I chose when Denna and I arrived, I slam the door shut like a petulant child in need of a time out. This can't be my future. There has to be another way, I thought as a plan of escape quickly unfurls in my mind. Knowing I'll have to wait until Preema and Denna are both asleep before I put my plan in motion, I repack my backpack.

I don't know how long I wait for the lodge to fall silent before I decide it's time to make my escape. Slipping on my Converse sneakers, I toss my backpack over my shoulder and make my way to the front door. Just as my hand reach out to open the door, I remember Denna setting the alarm system. Once I've disarmed the perimeter alarm, I step outside. The predawn air of the forest caress my skin, and I breathe in my first taste of freedom.

Racing as quickly as I can to get as far away as I can before the Council of Elders is made aware of my escape, I keep moving. I know I've run at least twenty-miles before I stop to catch my breath. Tired and unfamiliar with my surroundings, I miss the sound and the scent of a shifter advancing towards me until it's too late. Then all at once, Langdon's familiar musk is everywhere.

"How nice of you to come to me," he growls, stalking towards me.

I'd hope I was safe locked away, and hidden from the unmated males of my clan, especially this ruthless beta who has apparently been tracking me all along. Regaining my senses, I back away from the predator I have no chance of reasoning with.

"It's only a matter of time before I defeat your father. However, I have no problem with stacking the odds in my favor. I intend to be the one to claim your heat, omega. So, even if your father manages to prevail during the alpha challenge you'll still be mine."

Turning to run, I'm not fast enough when Langdon pounces on me, pinning me to the ground. Large hands claw at me attempting to remove my jeans. Instinctively, I fight back refusing to give into my rising heat. The fact that Langdon thinks he can force the alpha-omega bond enrages me more than his assumption that I'm his to claim regardless of the outcome of the alpha challenge.

I don't know if the fire boiling my blood is my own heat escalating or rage. However, when I reach out to grab a large stone nearby, I know rage has won. With as much force as I can muster without shifting, I crash the stone against Langdon's head twice before he slumps forward. The weight of his unconscious body falling against my chest steals the air from my lungs, and for a moment I panic. Once I manage to shove him off me, I check his breathing, satisfied he's still alive I grab my backpack and run.

• • • •

IT'S BEEN TWO DAYS of constantly looking over my shoulders for Langdon and the Council of Elders. Two days of hiding in the forest by night, traveling farther away from Sheridan Springs by day and two days of full-blown heat overtaking my mind and body.

Tonight the pouring rain batters my skin, soaking me to the bone. Stumbling aimlessly through the dense forest, I'm too exhausted to go any further, but I force my feet to keep moving. It's not until my legs are ready to give out that I spot a cabin in the distance. With a burst of renewed energy, I race towards shelter, seeking refuge from the downpour. Reaching the door, I sniff the air, before banging against it loudly. When no one answers, I enter the cabin cautiously to confirm it's empty.

Searching the cabin, I allow my shifter's sight to guide me. Although the cabin is empty now, there are signs that it's well maintained. Finding a lantern and a box of matches in the small living area, I light it and continue my exploration. My stomach rumbles at the sight of a wooden cupboard, and the hunger I've tried to ignore gives me an aching reminder. Hopeful strides carry me to the pantry, desperate to find something to ease my hunger. As luck or fate would have it, the cupboard isn't bare. Although the selection is limited to two cans of pork and beans, and a box of instant porridge, I thank the gods for my good fortune. Grabbing a can of beans, I peel the lid away and eat directly from the can, practically pouring the beans down my throat.

After wolfing down the second can of beans satisfies my hunger, the wet clothes clinging to me begs to be removed. With the lantern securely in my hand, I circle the small room shining light into the dark corners. Relief floods my veins, discovering a large unfinished pine bed tucked away in a corner on the opposite side of the room. Knowing that I'm truly alone gives me the courage to strip down to my bare skin. I peel away each wet layer of clothing and lay them out to dry. With my clothes spread out across the footboard of the bed, I climb under the covers. I manage to ignore the aching need between my thighs and fall asleep for a few uninterrupted and peaceful hours.

I don't know how long I've been sleeping when the sound of the door slamming shut, and a large looming shadow fills the small cabin startles me awake. Scenting another shifter, I scramble out of bed fearing Langdon or the Council of Elders have found me.

"What are you doing in my cabin?" The large male asks.

Offering a panic filled explanation, I say. "I was only seeking shelter from the rain. I thought the cabin was abandoned."

"What were you doing out in the rain? Did you get lost in the woods?" He asks from the shadows.

"What were you doing out in the rain?" I ask, tossing his question back at him.

"It's obvious you're a bear shifter," an omega in heat in fact."

Desperate to cover myself, I refuse to acknowledge his comments, instead I snatch my clothes from the footboard.

"Are you in some sort of trouble?"

"I'll leave your cabin as soon as I'm dressed," I say, stepping into my damp jeans.

"I thought you said, you needed shelter from the rain."

"What I need isn't your concern. I'll manage just fine on my own."

"Suit yourself."

Heavy footsteps stalk toward me, and in a moment of sheer panic my claws extend preparing for a fight. When the male strides pass me, a captive breath escapes my lungs. I watch him open the bedside table drawer and pull out a large black flashlight. Once he turns it on, bright light illuminates the room far better than the lantern had. Unable to look away, I stare at his back as he exits the cabin, taking the light with him. Bathe in darkness once again, I finish dressing quickly. After pulling my T-shirt over my head and stepping into my soggy Converse sneakers, I'm ready to leave just as light fills every corner of the cabin.

The door swings open moments later, and I get a good look at the male standing before me. The look in his moonlit eyes cause a surge of heat to race throughout my entire body. Aware that I'm in full blown heat, I back away before I make the worse mistake of my life.

"Is this your first heat?" He asks casually.

Nodding, I take a few more steps back, until I've backed myself into a corner. My bear grumbles, as if she's laughing at me. I know there's something about this male that calls to my bear. Something my inexperience mind isn't allowing me to see. As the last omega of my clan, I was always sheltered by my father. Although I've been in the presence of male shifters before, the Council of Elders forbid me to date, therefore I wasn't allowed to be anywhere near unmated male shifters. That is until two days ago.

"Why aren't you with your clan?"

"Because I want to be more than just a breeder for the next alpha," I snap.

"What do you want to be."

I'm caught off guard by his question because no one has ever asked me what I want. And the truth is I have no freaking clue. I've never allowed myself to even imagine freedom until I took it for myself.

"I don't know. I just know I want the opportunity to find out. So, I..."

"So, you decided to run away," he says, finishing my sentence.

"Something like that."

Changing the subject he asks, "Are you hungry?"

He follows my gaze to the discarded cans of beans, and my stomach chooses this moment to answer for me.

"If you want to stay for breakfast, I don't mind sharing," he says by way of an invitation.

Deciding that it's best to start the next leg of my journey with a full stomach, I accept. I follow behind him cautiously to a wood burning stove near the door. When he stops to pull out a large blue and white flannel shirt and a pair of white tube socks from a large duffle bag I didn't notice until now, I come to a stop a foot or so behind him.

"You may as well clean up and let your clothes dry while you're waiting," he says, offering me the shirt and socks.

Hesitantly, I reach for the dry clothing only to withdraw my hand. Tucking my hands behind my back, I struggle with my inner bear nudging me to give into my heat.

Zipping the duffle bag, he lays the clothing on top of it. "If you change your mind there here," he says before busying himself with meal prep.

Not sure what to do next, I stand in the middle of the room watching a stranger, another bear shifter prepare breakfast for me. When I make the mistake of looking at myself, the sight of my dirty clothes, and the not so pleasant stench that thankfully only I can smell due to my heat blocking the odor, makes my decision to accept the male's generosity more appealing.

Snagging the clothing from atop the duffle bag, I scurry away quickly before I change my mind.

"The bathroom is around the corner from the bed," he calls out.

Finding the bathroom easily, I step inside and lock the door. With just a small sink, a toilet and a shower, it may as well be a five-star spa. Kicking off my sneakers, I wiggle my toes against the plush rug beneath my bare feet. Eager to remove my damp dirty clothes, I peel off my water heavy jeans, my thin cotton T-shirt and dingy underwear.

Under the spray of hot water, I feel some of the tension leave my body. Unfortunately a hot shower does nothing to quell my raging heat. When the urge to touch myself becomes overwhelming, I climb out of the shower.

I dry my body with the only towel hanging on the rack, before slipping on the oversized flannel shirt. In an attempt to cover every part of my body, I button the shirt up to my neck. The shirt reaches pass my calves, but thankfully the socks will cover the rest of my legs. Hoping the bodywash along with a heavy spray of the male's cologne will mask the scent of my heat, I step out of the bathroom.

Entering the living area, I'm hit with the enticing scent of the male shifter and bacon. My bear takes notice, and I'm not sure which one she wants more. I get my answer when he turns to face me. The heat I see in his gaze rivals the heat between my thighs.

"Breakfast is ready," he says with a low core melting growl.

"Thank you."

Taking a seat at the small table near the wood burning stove, I wait for him to join me. When he places a dish of bacon, eggs and fried potatoes before me but refuses to sit with me, I force the food pass my lips.

"I want to share my heat with you." The words come out in a rush, but once they're out I don't regret saying them.

"You're under the influence of your heat, you have no idea what you're asking of me."

"I'm not asking you to become my mate. I want my first time to be with someone I choose. No, that's not right, I need my first time to be with someone I've chosen for myself."

"And what will you do when your heat returns?"

"Let me worry about what happens later, all I'm asking for is now."

Silence fills the cabin, and for a mortifying few seconds, I fear his rejection.

"Come here, Goldie."

Hearing him call me by the nickname only my father has ever used, I nearly lose my nerve. I shake all thoughts of my father from my head, and I stand. On unsteady legs, I place one foot in front of the other until I'm standing before him.

"No more hiding," he says, unbuttoning my borrowed shirt.

His fingers glide between my breast, and I moan enjoying the sudden contact. And when his large hands cup each of my breast and pinch my nipples, the pain ramps up my heat and amplifies my pleasure. The soulful dark brown eyes of his bear peeks out, inviting mine to join him.

No longer denying my heat, I allow myself to get carried away in a lustful passion induced haze. I give into what it means to be an omega. Desperate to share my heat, I let the unbutton shirt fall down my shoulders. Stepping closer to him, I push up on my tiptoes to reach his lips. I'm not sure what to expect for my first kiss, but heart stopping, and toe curling describes it best. His teeth nip at my bottom lip, forcing my mouth to open, and I welcome the invasion of his tongue. Moans give way to growls as he kisses me until I'm breathless. Even if kissing him meant this would be the last breath I take, I still wouldn't stop.

My heat sets me on fire from deep within my core, and I paw at his body eager to feel his skin against mine. Suddenly, he ends our kiss and steps away from me, and without thinking I follow him.

"Please don't stop, " I beg.

"I'm not stopping," he assures me. "I want to feel all of you pressed against me.

Standing before me, he undresses quickly, revealing his entire body to me. I gape at the size of him fully naked. His massive cock hangs long and hard, and the sight of it has my heat building to an inferno. Strong arms wrap around me, lifting me off my feet and instinctively my legs circle his waist. The taunt muscles of his abs tease the ache between my thighs. Unable to ignore my need, I grind my clit against the hard peaks of his stomach.

We tumble into bed locked in an embrace that refuses to be broken. And when his cock pushes pass my tight entrance, targeting the source of my need, I show my eagerness. My hips move frantically urging him to sink deeper. Thrust after thrust he fills me, hitting the spot that has my growls of pleasure rattling the cabin walls.

Our bodies find a rhythm that allows us to move in sync. Hard and fast we collide, taking what we need from each other. My mind and body accepts our union willingly, and before I realize what's happening it's too late. His knot swells inside me, locking us together, and as his knot takes hold of me, he claims my first orgasm.

I gasp as uncontrollable waves of pleasure shatters my soul. And when he growls his own pleasure, my body responds to his unspoken command for more. The inferno blazing between us becomes an unstoppable force demanding release. And the inevitable explosion that follows as we combust at the same time is overwhelming. His seed fills me, and my core spasms around his cock satiating my inherent need as an omega to breed.

After nearly forty-eight hours locked in a heat induced mating, I awake in bed alone. Climbing out of bed, I find my clothes clean and hanging across the footboard. Guilt batters my senses as I realize what I've done in the name of freedom. I've shamed my father, defied the Council of Elders, assaulted an alpha challenger, given my first heat and virginity to a stranger, and unintentionally triggered the mate bond. Knowing I have no other choice, I get dressed, leave the sanctuary of the cabin behind, and keep running.

Chapter 1
Rylie

SINCE ARRIVING IN WESTWOOD three and a half years ago, I've befriended a witch, Naomi Morgan, and her mate, Joseph Santana, a wolf shifter and his pack. To say I was drawn to Westwood would be an understatement. However, since learning that the small town is under the protection of a hybrid witch-wolf and her three fated mates made my decision to plant roots here easy, especially once Naomi found a way to suppress my heat. Unfortunately, the witch's potion didn't take away the memories of the bear shifter I shared my first heat with.

Although I feel relatively safe among the wolf shifters, witches and humans of Westwood, I'm still fearful that someday my clan will find me. I'm fearful they will discover my secret. Fortunately without the burden of my heat tracking me will be difficult.

Living mostly off the grid simplifies things down to my core needs, food and shelter. Once I learned how to survive on my own I was able to build a life for myself away from my clan. It took some time, but I even managed to obtain my nursing degree at Westwood Community College, with the help of my new found family. I know I would've never had the opportunities I have now if I had stayed in Sheridan Springs.

Tonight I'm finishing up the nightshift at Westwood Medical Center, and although my patients are humans some of them have beastly attitudes. With Miss Palmer being the exception. Checking her vitals, and administering her meds, I find myself chanting a spell to ease the elderly woman's pain. As a nurse there isn't anything I can do to rid her of the disease slowly claiming her life, but as a witch's apprentice, I can help her get a good night's sleep free of pain.

My ability to use magic has grown over the past year thanks to Naomi. Magic is in her blood, as a descendant of a powerful wolf-witch, magic comes easy for her. So when she offered to help me tap into the alpha-omega magic I inherited from my parents, the magic needed to preserve my clan, I agreed eagerly. And although my magic is taught, knowing the right spell makes all the difference.

Returning to the nurse's station after attending to my last patient, I check the clock against the wall ticking down the last two minutes of a ten-hour shift. When the clock strikes 6:00 a.m., I'm ready to bid the hospital goodbye for the next three days. Wearily, I make my way to the nurses lounge to grab my tote bag from my locker.

My home is a twelve-minute drive from the medical center. The fact that there's never any rush hour traffic, I always arrive home in time to make breakfast for Lorelei and Logan, my three-year-old cubs.

Working a four-day ten-hour evening shift has some advantages that works for me as a single mom. I get to tuck them in at night before I leave for work, I'm home before breakfast, and I'm able to drop them off at daycare, so I can get a few hours of sleep before family time, dinner and bath time. It's not ideal, but the three consecutive days off definitely helps. I'm also grateful for Symone, my roommate and fellow nurse who has become a sister to me, and auntie Sym, to my cubs.

The cozy two-bedroom cabin home, I rent from Naomi is half way between the hospital and the center of town. Parking my thirteen-year-old gray Honda CR-V, next to Symone's shiny blue Jeep Cherokee, has me feeling a little inadequate as I step out onto the graveled driveway.

Entering my home at nearly 7:30 in the morning it's still peacefully silent. I make my way to my bedroom, the larger of the two. Moving quietly about the room so as not to wake Logan and Lorelei, I tiptoe pass the sitting area I converted into a nursery for them. I don't fight the urge to take a peek at them. Kneeling between two toddler beds, I give them each a kiss on the forehead before heading to the shower.

After washing away the scent I've come to associate with the hospital, I feel clean and refreshed. By eight o'clock, Symone and I converge on the kitchen at the same time. Brewing her favorite cup of morning tea, she greets me.

"Good morning," she says, lifting her tea cup from the Keurig.

Returning her greeting, I reply. "Good morning, did the twins give you any trouble last night?"

Her smile is warm and genuine when she says. "Not a peep."

Nodding my gratitude, I ask. "Are you joining us for breakfast?"

"I don't have time this morning, I have to run an errand before my shift starts at nine."

"Okay, what about dinner?"

"I'm not sure, I might stop by Santana's for happy hour."

"Sounds like fun."

"I'll let you know either way," she chuckles.

After finishing her cup of tea, Symone handwash the delicate floral blue tea cup that once belonged to her great-grandmother and places it back in the cupboard before leaving for work. Hearing the front door close behind Symone makes me grateful to have her as a roommate. When she agreed to move in, she also agreed to help me with child care. Since we're on opposite shifts at the hospital we have a routine that works for us. And with the absence of a social life just like me, she's able to take care of Logan and Lorelei on the nights I work.

The pitter patter of little feet announce the arrival of my twins as they approach the kitchen. Logan enters first, holding his sister's hand as she trails sleepily behind him. Although Lorelei was born first, older than her brother by four minutes, Logan has always been her protective big brother.

"Mommy!" he greets excitedly.

Bending down, I welcome my son into my arms with a tight hug. "Good morning, Moonbeam."

At the mention of his nickname, Logan's gray expressive eyes shine bright. Seeing the eyes of his father staring up at me makes me wonder what could have been if I hadn't left that cabin. Over the years I thought about returning to the place my cubs were conceived, hoping that by some miracle their father is still there waiting for me.

"Mommy, I want a hug too," Lorelei says, rubbing the sleep from her eyes.

"Come here, Sunshine."

She giggles, and the perfect mini replica of me steps forward. Logan gives way to his sister, allowing her to receive her good morning hug. After giving them each a tender kiss on the forehead, I lead them to the breakfast table. A bowl of porridge topped with fresh berries awaits them along with a glass of milk. Logan is the first to dig in, lifting an overflowing spoon to his mouth.

"How is it, Moonbeam?"

"Just right, Mommy," he says around a mouthful of porridge.

"No talking with food in your mouth, Logan," Lorelei chastises.

"And how is yours, Sunshine?"

"Good, Mommy," she replies after swallowing down her first mouthful.

Joining them at the table with a cup of coffee and a blueberry muffin, I listen intently as one after the other seeks my attention.

"Mommy, why does Kota have three dads?"

I nearly choked while swallowing my coffee, at the mention of his playmate Dakota Westwood. The first-born son of Aria Morgan, the hybrid witch-wolf and the alpha queen to the Westwood wolf shifter pack. She's mated to Calian Westwood, the alpha king and the eldest of the Westwood triplets. He's also Dakota's biological father. However, Aria is also mated to Calian's brothers, Anakin and Kai who are alphas as well. Although omegas are often breeders to multiple alphas, we have never shared a mate bond with more than one alpha. The fact that Aria has three fated mates still comes as a shock to me, but I guess it's a wolf thing.

"Where is my daddy, Mommy?" Lorelei asks, pushing her empty bowl aside.

Caught between a rock and a hard place, I decide it's time for a distraction. Because there's no way I'm discussing the intricacies of fated mates with my three-year-old cubs. And I'm definitely not ready to explain the fact that their father has no idea they even exist.

"Who wants to go on a picnic and swimming at the waterfall today?"

"Me! Me!" They squeal in unison.

"Great, lets finish our breakfast, and after mommy has ran a few errands we can spend the afternoon at the waterfall."

"Yay! Logan cheers, while Lorelei claps happily.

Declaring today Friday Funday, I decide to forego taking the twins to daycare, instead they will accompany me while I run errands. Once the twins are secured in their car seats we're ready for a day of fun.

Our first stop is Naomi's herbal shop. It's time to replenished the herbs I used to block the scent of my omega pheromones and suppress my heat. Since giving birth to my cubs three years ago, a combination of herbs and a little witchcraft has kept my status as an omega bear shifter a secret. Most importantly it has kept my clan from finding me.

Coming to a stop outside Naomi's Herbal Shop, I park, and we head inside. Over the years Naomi has become a cherished friend and the mother I never knew I needed. Six months after the twins were born I experienced my heat for the second time. Alone and with two cubs to care for, I called on the one person I trusted to help me. Naomi didn't hesitate to come to my aid. As an herbalist she was able to use a variety of plants found in nature to ease my suffering. And when she taught me how to blend the herbs myself into a cup of tea along with an incantation to suppress my heat and block my scent, I knew I'd found the freedom I've craved all my life.

The moment we enter the shop Logan and Lorelei can't hide how happy they are to see Naomi.

"Omi!" Lorelei exclaims, pulling her hand free of my hold.

"Lorelei!" Naomi responds with equal enthusiasm.

I watch as she scoops my daughter up into her arms and pepper her rosy cherub cheeks with kisses. Lorelei's giggles are infectious, causing a few of Naomi's customers to smile warmly at the exchange.

"My turn, Omi." Logan pouts, and I assume he's a bit jealous of the attention his sister is receiving at the moment.

Giving Lorelei one final kiss on the cheek, Naomi place her feet firmly on the floor before turning her attention to Logan.

"Your turn," Naomi says, lifting Logan into her arms while pretending he's too heavy. "I'm not sure I can hold up such a big boy."

"I'm not too big for hugs and kisses, Omi," Logan declares.

"No you're not," Naomi agrees, hugging him tightly and kissing his cheeks with the same enthusiasm she shared with Lorelei.

When Logan's giggles give way to hiccups, Naomi whispers a spell to quiet them before releasing him.

"We're doing errands with Mommy today," Lorelei volunteers.

"And then we're going to the waterfall for a picnic, "Logan adds.

"And swimming too," Lorelei continues.

"That sounds like a lot of fun, I hope you're not too tired to come to the fair tomorrow."

At the mention of the Westwood Founders Day Fair, I'm reminded of my road trip to Chesterfield. The timing couldn't have been better, with the twins safe in Westwood with Naomi and Santana, I can make the trip to see my father.

"We won't be tired." The twins chime in unison.

"Good," Naomi cheers. "Now let's take care of your mommy's errand so you can get to the fun stuff." Taking the twins by the hand, Naomi leads us to her office.

Entering the office the first thing I see is the large 18th century mahogany Apothecary cabinet Naomi use for storing and organizing her herbal remedies.

"Go ahead and grab what you need," Naomi instructs.

"Thank you."

Finding the ingredients required to suppress my heat and block the scent of my omega pheromones, I take what I need. Over the past year I've learn to mix herbs for healing and spiritual cleansing, as well as memorizing several spells and incantations for protection to keep myself and the twins safe.

"Can we go see Santa, Mommy?" Logan asks with a hint of boredom in his voice.

"As soon as we're done here, Moonbeam."

"I'll let him know you're stopping by with the kids." Naomi says, offering me a bag to carry the herbs I've collected.

"Thanks, one day I'll remember to bring my tote bag," I quip.

"As long as you remember to bring my cuddle bears, I'll supply the bags," Naomi replies happily.

Returning her smile, I agree before facing Lorelei and Logan.

"Who's ready to go see Santa?"

"Me!" They exclaim.

"I guess we're off to our next stop," I say, leaning in for a quick hug from Naomi.

Escorting us from her office, Naomi stops to answer a question from one of her many customers. Although the townspeople, more specifically the humans, gossip about Naomi being a witch, they don't know the true scope of her powers, or the magic inherit to the Morgan witches. As we making our way to the exit, a woman in tears enters the store.

"Thanks again for this," I say, lifting the bag of herbs. "I think you're expertise is needed."

"It certainly looks that way."

"Bye Omi," Lorelei says, waving to Naomi.

"Hug and kisses, cuddle bears," she says before coming to the aid of the crying woman.

After stopping at Santana's for a quick visit, and a picnic basket filled with the perfect feast for my growing cubs, the twins and I head to Westwood Falls. The waterfall is a sixty-footlong channel between narrow deep-orange travertine cliffs with shimmering aqua-blue water spilling over and pooling at the bottom of a small canyon.

"Mommy, can I swim now?" Logan asks, eager to dive into the water.

"Wait for us, Moonbeam," I instruct, taking Lorelei by the hand.

Since arriving I've discovered the magic of Westwood isn't just its people, it's also hidden treasures like the waterfall, a sanctuary for my cubs and me to picnic and swim on a long hot day. Westwood has become a safe haven, a place I can finally call home.

Chapter 2
Rylie

AFTER BREAKFAST SATURDAY morning, I drop Logan and Lorelei off at Naomi and Santana's place. They have agreed to take the twins to the Westwood Founders Day Fair, leaving me worry free to drive to Chesterfield for a visit with my father.

Since the day my twins were born Naomi and Santana have been gifts from the gods. As honorary grandparents they're a true blessing. They're also the reason, I feel confident driving over one hundred miles to meet my father for lunch. I know my cubs are in safe hands with a powerful witch and wolf shifter looking after them while I'm away.

The drive to Chesterfield is uneventful, and when I arrive at Mae Belle's diner my father is there to greet me. He escorts me to our usual table, and I slide into the booth, taking the seat across from him. The summer heat and the lack of air conditioning causes the blood red vinyl seat to stick to the back of my thighs. Regretting my decision to wear my favorite denim skirt, I make an awkward attempt to free myself.

"Here, use this," my father says, offering his handkerchief.

After placing the handkerchief between my thighs and the vinyl seat, I feel better instantly.

"Thank you," I manage to say as the waitress appear to take our lunch order.

"What can I get you folks today?"

Not bothering to look at the menus, my father and I order our usual, bacon cheeseburgers and onion rings, with a strawberry milkshake for me and a chocolate shake for him. My father and I have been meeting at Mae Belle's diner for the past six months. Once I decided to reach out to him, I knew meeting in Sheridan Springs wasn't an option. And since I'm not ready to invite him to my home in Westwood, Chesterfield became neutral grounds for our monthly lunch date.

"How have you been since we last spoke?" My father asks, unable to hide the worry in his voice.

"I swear to you, I'm well. I'm safe and I have people in my life that care about me."

"Then why all the secrecy? Reaching across the table, my father take my hand in his. "Why are you still hiding, Rylie?"

"Because I won't make it easy for the Whitmores and the Council of Elders to find me," I snap. "I refuse to become a breeder for an alpha I loathe and a clan I want no part of."

"There has to be a better way, Rylie."

"Not as long as the Council of Elders continue to enforce archaic breeding laws."

"Our laws are the reason our clan still exists. The shifter magic of the alpha-omega bond insures our clan's survival."

"Our clan hasn't had a true alpha-omega mate bond for more than a hundred years. That's the real reason the Sheridan Springs bear clan's shifter magic is diminishing."

"Your mother and I weren't fated mates, but we performed our duties as alpha and omega for the sake of the clan."

"And had I been born an alpha instead of an omega, you wouldn't have been challenged and the Council of Elders wouldn't have the power to force me to become a breeder."

"So instead you deny who you truly are with a witch's potions and spells?"

"I've never denied I'm an omega. However, I do choose not to let being an omega define me."

Before my father voices a response the waitress returns with our meals. "Enjoy," she says, placing our plates of food on the table.

I watch my father take two big bites of his bacon cheeseburger, stuffing his mouth full. I take that as a sign our discussion regarding the clan is over. For now at least. An uncomfortable silence falls between us as I attempt to choke down the food I no longer have an appetite for.

An hour after the worse lunch date my father and I have since we began meeting six months ago comes to an end; he escorts me to my car.

"Drive safe," he says planting a kiss on my cheek and shutting my car door before walking away.

Leaving Mae Belle's behind, I notice a black pickup truck following me from the parking lot. My anxiety kicks into overdrive seeing the Utah license plate in my rearview mirror. The thought of being followed back to Westwood cause my palms to sweat and my heart to race frantically.

When the truck continues to follow me for several miles, I use my iPhone to dictate license plate number B674TP to Siri. I'm hoping this is all just a big coincidence, but better safe than sorry. Desperate to know if I'm being followed, I come to a stop at a gas station hoping to lay my doubts to rest.

From behind the wheel of my car, I watch as the vehicle continues on pass me. Breathing a sigh of relief releases me from my fear, and I take a moment to thank whatever deity that continues to look out for me.

• • • •

IT TAKES LONGER THAN I originally planned to reach Westwood. When I arrive, I'm eager to set my eyes on the twins. Parking my car near Westwood Town Hall, I begin walking the two blocks to Forrest Grove park, the site of the fair. The park is named after architect, Forrest Blackcloud, who also happens to be the father of the Westwood triplets, Calian, Anakin and Kai.

Entering the park, Symone is the first familiar face I see in the crowd. With quick strides I catch up to her at one of the concession stands buying popcorn.

"You made it," Symone greets as I approach.

"Barely," I reply before she hands me a small bag of popcorn.

"That's for Lorelei," she says by way of explanation.

Nodding, I follow her to the next stand where she buys a mound of cotton candy.

"And this is for Logan."

"You're spoiling them," I chastise gently.

"That's what aunties are for. I stuff them with treats, and you take care of the upset tummies."

Since shifters tend not to come down with human illnesses, I'm fairly certain I can handle a tummy ache or two.

"I guess it's a good thing auntie Symone is also a nurse."

Laughing, Symone leads me away from the concession stands to a picnic blanket near a large oak tree. Logan is the first to see us approaching.

"Mommy!" he shouts, racing towards us.

The sound of my son's giggles warm my heart. Bending to reach him, I scoop him up into my arms.

"Hello, my moonbeam, I've missed you," I say, while covering his cherub cheeks with kisses.

"I missed you too, Mommy."

"Are you having fun with Omi and Santa?"

"And auntie Sym," Symone chimes.

"Lots and lots of fun," Logan replies, reaching for Symone and his cotton candy.

Handing Logan over to Symone, she gives him the fluffy concoction and he doesn't hesitate to take a huge bite.

"Lead the way, little man," Symone says, placing Logan firmly on his feet.

Running back to join the others on the picnic blanket, Logan shouts. "Look what auntie Sym got me."

"I'm glad you made it back in time to see the fireworks," Naomi says, as I take a seat beside her on the blanket.

I try to hide the rush of panic, but Naomi hears it in my tone when I say. "I almost didn't."

Clasping my hand in hers, she gives it a gentle squeeze before releasing it.

"Tell me about it later."

Nodding, I turn my attention to Lorelei. "Hello, Sunshine."

Instead of the greeting I've come to expect from my daughter, she says, "Mommy, tell Logan cotton candy is not a good for you snack."

"It's good to my tummy," Logan teases.

"Yuck," Lorelei responds scrunching her nose.

"Your popcorn is yucky," Logan retaliates.

"Logan, would you like to go play with Dakota before the fireworks start?"

I'm grateful when Santana offers a distraction to end the twins bickering. However, Lorelei isn't easily distracted. "You're yucky," she pouts.

"Can we ride the pony?" Logan asks, his cheerful disposition returning as he ignores his sister's comment.

"Only if it's okay with your mom, and Kota's mom and dad."

"Mommy, can I? Please please please."

"Yes, you may go ride the pony with Kota if his parents allow it."

"Thank you, Mommy."

"You're welcome, Moonbeam."

"Let's go see my grandson," Santana says extending his hand.

With his cotton candy nearly finished, Logan accepts Santana's offered hand.

"Mommy."

"Yes, Sunshine."

"I want a twin sister."

Lorelei's statement catch me off guard, and it renders me dumbstruck for unbearably long seconds.

"It's too late for you to have a twin sister because twin babies are born together. They share the same birthday just like you and Logan."

"But Logan doesn't like to play with me."

When my little ray of sunshine begins to sniffle, I know she's trying to be a big girl. Pulling her onto my lap, I give her a tight hug, holding her until I find the right words to console her.

"You and your brother were each other's first best friend, and you still are."

"Logan said Kota is his best friend."

"It's okay to have more than one best friend."

"Do you have a best friend, Mommy?"

Growing up in Sheridan Springs, I never had much of an opportunity to make friends. As a child I wasn't allowed to play with the children of my clan because as the only omega, I had to be sheltered from harm. And as I grew older things only got worse, I wasn't allowed to socialize with my female peers, or be anywhere near unmated male shifters.

However, since moving to Westwood, I can truthfully say, I now have two best friends. Extending my hand to Naomi and Symone, I smile as they stack their hand atop mine.

"I have two best friends, Sunshine."

Smiling she says, "Omi and auntie Sym."

"That's right. So you see, it's okay to have two best friends."

"Can I go ride the pony with Logan and Kota?"

"I think that's a great idea."

"Can Omi and auntie Sym come too?"

"Best friends stick together," Symone says.

"Yes we do," Naomi chimes.

After several pony rides and another round of cotton candy, the kids were overly excited and ready for the fireworks to begin. When Kota's dad, Calian lifts him onto his shoulders, It didn't escape my notice that Logan's mood had changed. My normally carefree son is missing the presence of his own father.

Once again I'm thankful when Santana intervenes by lifting Logan onto his shoulders.

Gazing up at Logan, my eyes fill with unshed tears when the sound of my son's laughter erupts. As the night sky begin to twinkle with fireworks, I force myself to look away. Unfortunately, I'm unable to hide the sadness in my eyes from Santana.

"Thank you." I mouthed.

The smile I see in his eyes says everything his words can't at the moment.

We're family.

Chapter 3
Rylie

IT CAN BE HARD GETTING back into a daily routine, especially after a long three-day weekend. Unfortunately it doesn't help when your alarm clock fails to go off. With less than an hour to get the twins fed and dressed before dropping them off at day care, I feel like I've forgotten something.

"Good morning, kiddos," Symone says, entering the kitchen.

Making a beeline to the twins she gives them each a kiss on the forehead.

"Good morning, auntie Sym," they say in unison.

"I love it when you guys do that."

"Do what, auntie Sym?"

"That," she says chuckling. "When you both say the same thing at the same time."

"Mommy said that's our twin power," Lorelei replies.

"Are you going to have breakfast with us?" Logan asks.

"I'll make myself a cup of tea, and I'll sit with you while you have breakfast."

Symone retrieves her blue floral teacup and saucer from the cabinet before popping her favorite English Breakfast K-Cup in the Keurig.

"Mommy can I have a cup of tea with honey?"

"We don't have time this morning, Sunshine, mommy is running late."

Symone takes a seat at the breakfast table, sipping her tea, as the twins finish eating their breakfast. With Lorelei and Logan distracted by Symone, I finally get a chance to drink my cup of coffee. The lukewarm caffeine does little to boost my energy, and once again I try to recall what it is I've forgotten.

"All done, Mommy."

"I've got this," Symone says, collecting Logan and Lorelei's dirty dish.

"Thank you."

While Symone washes the dishes, I help the twins with their shoes, and within five minutes the four of us are out the door. Once again Symone comes to my rescue, securing Lorelei in her car seat. With both kids strapped in and ready to go, we say goodbye to Symone.

Running ten minutes late, I don't immediately notice the black pickup truck until it passes me on the road. However, when the driver turns around and starts speeding towards me the Utah license plate is hard to miss. Alarm bells start going off in my head, telling me loud and clear to get away. Telling me to keep my children safe.

Unfortunately, when I change lanes attempting to go around the driver, my tire suddenly blows out. I tell myself not to panic until the pep talk finally reaches my brains. Remembering to keep a tight grip on the steering wheel, I force myself not to hit the brakes.

Once I pull over onto the shoulder, I check to make sure all the doors are locked before reaching for my cell phone. My heart sinks discovering the battery is dead. And that's when it hits me, I forgot to charge my freaking cell phone last night.

"What's wrong, Mommy?" Logan asks.

"Mommy has a flat tire, but we're going to be okay, Moonbeam."

Hoping I'm able to keep my promise, I turn my attention back to the pickup truck, watching and waiting for the driver to make his next move. A moment later the driver's door swings open and large worn brown boots step out of the vehicle onto the pavement.

"Is he going to help us with the tire, Mommy?" Lorelei questions.

My response is caught in my throat, when a tall bear of a man walks up to my car and smash the window in with his fist. The glass shatters, and shards of the broken pieces hit my face. Pain pricks my scalp as he drags me by my hair from the car and shove me down onto the ground.

"You belong with a clan, omega," he growls, and I hear his beast's disdain.

"Mommy, I don't like the bad man," Lorelei cries.

"Looks like I'm getting a two for one omega special today."

"Don't you touch my daughter."

Laughing at his own distasteful joke, he ignores me and attempts to open the back passenger door.

"Or what, omega."

Unable to cage my bear any longer, I let the shift happen to protect my cubs. The bones in my body break and contort, slowly changing me from woman to beast. When my painful growls steal his attention away from Lorelei, my bear peers into the darkness of his soulless eyes.

"So the little blonde omega bear wants to challenge me," he taunts.

Dropping to all fours, he shifts quickly and effortlessly, attacking me before I've fully shifted. Fighting back, I push pass the pain, and manage to land a blow to his abdomen. Unfortunately, the cries of my cubs distract me, and the beast of a bear knock me to the ground. Large claws tear at my flesh unleashing unimaginable pain until the loss of blood defeats me.

• • • •

WAKING IN UNFAMILIAR surroundings isn't the best way to start the day. Then I remember, the black pickup truck, my painful shift, the fight, and oh my gods, Lorelei being taken. Wailing at the top of my lungs, I scream for help. Within seconds, Symone and a doctor I don't recognize come running into the room.

"He took my little girl," I say between bouts of heart wrenching sobs. "He took her."

"Try to calm down, Rylie. You were in a car accident, but you're going to be okay."

Symone tries to soothe me, but the bear I uncage can't be consoled, all she wants to do is hunt down the person that took her cub. "

"I need to find my little girl," I manage to say through sniffles.

"Where is Lorelei, Ms. Adams? What did you do to her?"

The accusation I hear in the doctor's voice is clear. He believes I'm responsible for Lorelei being missing. Symone gives the doctor a chastising look before taking my hand in hers.

"Rylie," Symone says, drawing my attention away from the doctor. "This is Dr. Thomas Taylor, he's a child psychologist. We brought him in to speak with Logan."

"Logan, what's happened to my son?"

"Logan is fine, he's sleeping. But he has apparently experienced a traumatic event."

"I need to see my son."

"Your son is saying you turned into a monster and the monster took Lorelei away."

Once again the doctor's word are accusatory, even if he only has half of the story right. Guilt and shame battle for dominance, as I come to terms with everything my children have witnessed. If I had prepared the twins for what it means to be a shifter, seeing me change wouldn't have been a traumatic experience for Logan.

"What do you have to say for yourself, Ms. Adams?" Dr. Thomas asks.

Before I have an opportunity to respond, a stern looking woman enters the room.

"You won't be seeing your son until this issue is resolved."

"And who are you to tell me I can't see my son?" I growl.

"I'm Kristine Frances, I work for Child Protective Services, and I've been assigned to Logan's case. Based on Dr. Thomas's report and my own interview with your son, he witnessed you turning into a monster and the monster took his sister away."

Defending myself, I say, "I would never hurt my children."

"Yet your daughter is missing, and your son believes you're the reason. So you can see why I can't allow you to influence Logan's version of the story."

Unable to explain the event that led up to my daughter's kidnapping, I keep quiet.

"Rylie, they're only here to help,"

Pulling my hand free of Symone's hold, I reply, "They can't help me."

"You're absolutely correct, Ms. Adams, CPS can't help you if you don't cooperate. However, we can remove Logan from your home until this case has been investigated fully."

The threat hangs in the air suffocating me with each of Ms. Frances's venomous words.

"You can't take my son away from me!" I shout.

"With no family in town to take care of your son, I have no choice."

"He can stay with me," Symone suggests.

"That's not possible when you and Ms. Adams are roommates. However, Ms. Adams, if you have someone else we can place Logan with temporarily it will be better for him."

"Will you allow Logan to stay with his godparents?" I plea.

"If they are willing to take him, his godparents is an acceptable option."

"I'll call them," Symone says, retrieving her cell phone from her pocket before leaving the room.

"Am I free to go?"

"I can't place you under arrest, Ms. Adams, however, the sheriff's department may have other ideas regarding your freedom, so I suggest you seek legal counsel. "

"Until then I have nothing more to say, so you can both leave now."

Symone returns, as Dr. Thomas and Ms. Frances are leaving.

"Were you able to reach Logan's godparents?" I hear Ms. Frances ask.

"Yes, they're on their way to pick up Logan. They should be here soon."

The door closes after Symone enters the room fully. Climbing out of bed, I search the small wardrobe for my clothes. When I find it empty, I turn to Symone for answers.

"Where are my clothes?"

"They've been collected as evidence."

Unable to control my anger, I shout. "Evidence of what!"

"Your clothes were covered in blood and your daughter is missing, Rylie." Symone's harsh words belie the pity I see in her eyes. "You are being investigated; they think you..."

Symone didn't have to finish her sentence; I know what everyone thinks. They believe I've done something to harm my daughter.

"I didn't hurt Lorelei. I would never hurt my children. You have to believe me, Symone."

"If you didn't hurt her, where is she, Rylie?"

Symone's question only proves, I've failed to convince her of my innocence.

"Do you think I hurt Lorelei?"

"I don't know what to think. Your son is traumatized, and your daughter is missing. Something clearly happened to cause these two things."

"You wouldn't believe me if I told you." I mutter to myself.

Knowing I can't share my secret with Symone or any human, my only choice is to let them continue to believe the worst about me. Because why would they ever believe shifters exist, that one attacked me and kidnapped my daughter. Why would they believe that there are supernatural beings that walk among them every day when we have gone to extraordinary lengths to keep our existence a secret.

"You can trust me, Rylie, I only want to help."

"If you want to help me, get me a change of clothes so I can get out of here."

A tap at the door, has Naomi peeking her head in seconds later. Relief overwhelms me at the sight of the trust and love I see in her eyes. Instantly my bear calms sensing another being I'm able to share my truth with. Someone who can be of assistance with getting my daughter back.

"Please come in," I urge.

"I brought you a change of clothing," she says, handing over a small overnight bag.

"Thank you."

Although, I only uttered two words, I'm sure Naomi hears the depth of my true meaning. *Thank you for taking care of Logan. Thank you for bringing the clothes. Thank you for believing me. Thank you for your help.*

"Please excuse me while I get dressed."

From the privacy of the bathroom, I wash my hands and face, cleaning the residue of blood from my skin. After freshening up, I dress quickly in a pair of jeans and a white T-shirt. Returning to the bedroom to my relief I find Symone has left.

"I thought we needed some time alone to talk," Naomi says, explaining Symone's absence. "Start by telling me everything that happened."

"Before I do, please tell me how Logan is doing."

"He's scared the bad monster won't bring Lorelei back."

"Is he also scared of me?"

"He calls you the good monster. He said you tried to fight the bad monster, but he hurt you and took Lorelei away."

The struggle to regain my composure has me nodding my head frantically.

"Santana is taking him to Westwood Estate."

Releasing the breath trapped in my constricting lungs, I realize Logan is staying at the safest place possible. The Westwood Estate is home to a pack of alpha wolves and a powerful witch-wolf hybrid, who happens to be Santana's daughter, Aria.

"With everything going on we believe hanging out with Kota will be a good distraction for Logan." Naomi adds.

Fighting back unshed tears, I recount the ordeal, telling Naomi how the shifter practically ran us off the road, how my tire suddenly blew out, and how I shifted in front of the twins in order to protect them.

"I had trouble shifting, and unfortunately he was able to completely shift first. Not that it would've changed the outcome. He's a much stronger and larger bear than me. But I had to protect my cubs, so I kept fighting until I couldn't."

"He's the monster that took Lorelei," Naomi surmises.

"Yes." I choke out. "And I have to get her back."

"We will. I promise."

"How?"

"With the help of a few good friends. Now let's get out of here."

• • • •

NEARLY AN HOUR AFTER leaving the hospital, Naomi and I arrive at a rustic log cabin somewhere near Westwood Falls. Something about the cabin calls to me, something about it stirs my blood. I don't know if it's my bear or just being surrounded by nature.

Entering the cabin, I follow Naomi's lead. I take in every aspect of the cozy living area, everything from the wood burning stove to the large window with a view. My gaze continue to roam the room when I recognize the people in the photos. So many photos depicting a happy family. The most prominent person in each photo is Aria Morgan, Naomi's niece and mate to the Westwood triplets.

"Calian built this cabin for him and his brothers. But as you can see, Aria has added her touch to it as well."

Curious, I ask. "Why are we here?"

"This is where we're all meeting to discuss the best course of action to get Lorelei back."

"Who's meeting us here?"

"Everyone." Clarifying, Naomi says. "Santana, Aria, Calian, Anakin, Kai and the new sheriff, Creed Masterson.

"If Santana is meeting us, who's taking care of Logan?"

"Rosalie will be taking care of Logan and Dakota until we return to Westwood Estate."

Feeling more in control than I did a few hours ago, I accept my limitations and wait for the others to arrive. Lost in my own thoughts, I didn't hear Santana entering the cabin until he says.

"Aria and her mates are right behind me."

Eager to set a plan in motion to get Lorelei back, I dismiss the heat warming my veins for anger growing in my heart.

Breathing in and out, I attempt to clear my head of the muddled thoughts distracting me.

Calian Westwood steps into the cabin and my bear recognizes him as a powerful alpha immediately. As the alpha-king of the Westwood pack, this is his territory to rule. With Aria's hand securely in his, she follows close behind him. Anakin and Kai, bring up the rear, flanking Aria. Calian leads Aria to the small table, and Anakin pulls out a chair for her, but Aria remains standing. It still surprises me that all three shifters are her fated mates.

"We've done this before, my sweet," Anakin says.

"Yes, we have," Aria agrees, resting her hand protectively over her belly.

"So indulge us, little wolf," Calian adds.

It's not fair when you two gang up on me," she pouts.

In unison with heat flaring in their eyes, Aria's mates take predatory steps toward her. The passion they feel for her is palpable, it's as if they have forgotten they're not alone. Lifting Aria's chin to meet his gaze, Calian says, "I thought you liked when we gang up on you."

"Behave," she says when Kai, tugs at her hair.

"Yes, my queen," he whispers, forgetting that he's in a room with shifters with exceptional hearing.

Clearing his throat, Santana interrupts the scene, gaining the attention of Aria and her enamored mates.

"Congratulations," I say when the room falls silent for long intense seconds.

"Thank you," Aria returns graciously.

"Sweetheart, please stop torturing your mates and take a seat." Santana pleas.

"I guess the wolf's out of the bag now," she says, taking a seat at her father's insistence.

Now that Aria is settled, all eyes turn their focus to me. Compelled to say something, I start by thanking everyone.

"I want to thank you all for your help. I truly appreciate..."

"That must be Sheriff Masterson," Naomi says, when a knock at the door cuts me off.

Santana, who's closest to the door opens it. A large figure fills the door, blocking out the light. Unbidden, the memory of a rainy night long ago conjure images of a large looming shadow filling a small cabin in a similar way.

"Glad you could make it, sheriff," Santana greets.

"Glad to be of service."

Hearing the deep timbre of a voice I've never forgotten causes my core to spasm uncontrollably. And when he steps into the cabin my bear recognizes the scent of the shifter I thought I would never see again. Upon seeing me a deep growl leaves his throat. The sound reverberate throughout the small space, gaining the wolves attention. I don't know how long I stare into gray eyes that look so much like my son's, but when heavy footfalls stride toward me, I panic.

Taking a few cautious steps back, I turn to run away. Unfortunately, the route to my escape is blocked. With nowhere to run, I'm forced to face the consequences of my actions. Somehow, Naomi must have sensed my distress over the situation with the sheriff.

"Is there a problem?" She asks, her question laced with the concern of a mother.

"I need a moment to speak with the sheriff alone."

Silently questioning me, she nods. "Take as much time as you need."

"Will you follow me outside, please."

Without a word he follows me, shutting the door quietly behind him. Aware that all shifters have excellent hearing, I suggest a more private option.

"Do you mind if we talk inside your vehicle?"

Maintaining his silence, he opens the passenger door for me. I watch as he rounds the front of the vehicle to climb into the driver's seat. His massive frame sits stiffly as waves of tension coils his body. My brain struggles to find the right words, until I blurt out the first thing that comes to mind.

"My name is Rylie Adams."

Chapter 4
Creed

STARTING OVER IS NEVER easy, especially when the past continues to haunt you. However, the last place I expected to make a new beginning is in a town that is home to a wolf pack. As I approach the Welcome to Westwood sign, I come to an abrupt stop when the scent in the air awakes my bear from his slumber.

Once I manage to contain my bear, I straddle my motorcycle and enter wolf shifter territory. I continue riding until I reach Westwood Inn. The Inn consist of a main house, and several cabins nestled along the edge of the forest. Grabbing my duffle bag from the back of my motorcycle, I bound up the steps to the main house.

"Welcome to Westwood Inn," the Innkeeper, Maeve, according to her name tag greets me as I approach the reception counter.

"I'm Creed Masterson, I believe you have keys for me."

"Yes, I do, Mr. Masterson. As the town's new sheriff you've been given one of the larger more secluded cabins."

Nodding my appreciation, I wait for Maeve to retrieve the keys.

"Will Mrs. Masterson be joining you later?" When I didn't answer, Maeve continues with her not-so-subtle interrogation. "It's just that the two-bedroom cabins are usually reserved for families," she attempt to clarify before offering me the keys to the cabin.

After refusing to offer any insight into my private life, I accept the keys. Three keys total, one to the cabin, another for the vehicle assigned to the sheriff of Westwood, and another for the sheriff's office.

Exiting the Inn's main house, I follow the map to the cabin I'll call home for the foreseeable future. When I enter the rustic two-bedroom cabin, I can't help but think of the omega bear shifter who shared her heat with me.

It has been more than three years since I entered my cabin on a rainy night and found an omega in full heat sleeping in my bed. I remember how my body responded to the scent of her omega pheromones, and how it had taken every ounce of control I possess to resist going into rut and claiming her heat for myself on the spot.

Dropping my bag on the floor, I open the door to the private back porch, and step out into the night air hoping the sound of birds singing, the wind rustling between the trees of the forest and the water flowing from the waterfall nearby will distract me from memories I can't forget.

Under the glow of a full moon the restless beast I keep caged demands his freedom. It has been a few weeks since I let my bear roam free. Giving in to animal instincts, I undress quickly and relinquish control, urging the beast to come forward. As the shift begins my body contorts and my bones break reshaping themselves. With a fierce growl, the Kodiak I keep caged is set free. Standing over nine feet tall my bear peers into the darkness of the forest before dropping to the ground on all fours. Eager to explore new territory he races deep into the unknown.

I don't know how long I allow my bear to roam the forest before falling asleep. However, when I awake before sunrise in a cave miles away from the cabin, I know my bear has found his den and I need to be better prepared the next time.

Trekking bare ass naked through the forest is not exactly how I envisioned the start of my first official day as Westwood town sheriff. As luck or fate would have it, I make it back to the cabin without being seen. After a quick shower, I'm dressed and out the door once again.

From the cabin the commute to Westwood Town Hall is uneventful. Pulling into the parking spot reserved for the sheriff, I park the Ford Explorer effortlessly, before grabbing my Stetson and climbing out of the vehicle.

• • • •

I HAVEN'T BEEN ON THE job for more than two hours, before I'm being summoned to the home of Calian Westwood, whose ancestors founded the town of Westwood, to investigate the kidnapping of a three-year-old little girl.

On route to Westwood Estate I recieve a call from my deputy, informing me that the crime scene has been compromised with animal footprints. Apparently a bear wondered onto the sight before my deputy arrived.

The Estate is on fifteen thousand acres of private forest that belongs to the Westwood family. The house is nestled perfectly among the trees of the forest, complementing the natural landscape all around it.

Climbing out of my truck, purposeful strides carry me up the steps of a large wraparound porch to the front door. Before I have an opportunity to ring the doorbell it swings open.

"You must be Creed Masterson, our new sheriff?"

Lifting my Stetson from my head, I reply. "Yes Ma'am."

"Well it's nice to meet you sheriff. Please follow me, Calian has been waiting for you."

"Lead the way, Ma'am"

"I'm Rosalie by the way," she says as I enter the house.

I follow Rosalie, down a hall pass the large family room to a private office. Rising from his seat behind his desk, Calian Westwood offers me his hand in greeting.

"Thank you, Rosalie," Westwood says before she shuts the door.

Cutting to the chase, he gets to the point.

"There's no need to try to hide what we've already scented about each other. We're shifters, I'm a wolf and you're..."

"A bear," I acknowledge, cutting him off.

"Which is why I've called you here. A little girl was kidnapped by a shifter a few hours ago and I need your help to find her. I also need you to destroy any evidence that implicates the child's mother. She's a friend of the family and a bear shifter as well."

Remembering what my deputy said about animal footprints contaminating the crime scene, I understand his request for help.

"I'll do everything within my power to find the child but are you sure the mother isn't involved."

"I'm absolutely positive Rylie had nothing to do with this. "

"Then consider the evidence gone."

"Members of my pack are meeting with Rylie at my family's cabin, will you meet us there?"

"I'll meet you there after I've taken care of the evidence."

Escorting me to the door, Westwood gives me the directions to his family's cabin. After leaving the Estate, I return to the Sheriff's Department on a mission to destroy evidence in order to maintain the secret that shifters exist.

• • • •

WHEN I ARRIVE AT THE cabin, a familiar scent lingering in the air distracts me momentarily. Knocking on the door of the cabin, I'm greeted by a wolf shifter, I assume is a member of Westwood's pack.

"Glad you could make it, sheriff."

"Glad to be of service." I reply.

Stepping fully into the cabin, I immediately recognize the scent of my fated mate. Blue eyes meet mine, and I'm drawn into her oceanic depths unable to look away. Unable to resist the pull, I step towards her, only to have her attempt to retreat.

I hear the exchange of words between her and an older African American woman, but for the life of me I couldn't tell you what they said to each other. Her words finally register when she asks, "Will you follow me outside, please."

Wordlessly, I follow her outside, shutting the door behind me. When she suggests we speak inside my vehicle, I give her the privacy she requests.

Unable to find the right words to say to the mate I thought I would never see again, I remain silent. On autopilot, I open the passenger door for her before climbing into the driver's seat. Confined in such close proximity to her, my body aches desperately for hers.

"My name is Rylie Adams," she announces.

Her name echoes in my head, waking my bear. *Mine*, he growls from his cage, forcing me to take notice. *Mine*, I repeat to myself, allowing everything I know about my mate to sink in. She's an omega. She was in heat when we met nearly four years ago. She shared her first heat with me sending me into rut and together we unintentionally triggered the mate bond.

Holy fuck is it possible Rylie's kidnapped daughter is also mine. Needing to know the truth, I ask the question.

"Is she my daughter?"

Turning to face her, I wait for an answer that seem to take a lifetime. I've felt incomplete, for three long years knowing my mate had rejected me, now I need to know if she's denied me my child as well.

"Yes, Lorelei is your daughter."

Feeling the sting of her betrayal more deeply, I'm not sure how to respond. So, I stick to working the case for now.

"Do you have any idea who would want to take your child."

Nodding, she says, "My former clan."

"And which clan is that?"

"The Sheridan Springs clan."

My stomach lurch at the thought of my daughter being taken by a savage from the Sheridan Springs clan.

"Your daughter is an omega too?" I ask even though I already know the answer.

"Yes, she was born an omega."

"So that's why they want her, to breed her when she's older."

"It's what they wanted to do to me, and now they have my little girl."

Hearing Rylie break down in tears, I can tell she's been holding them back for a while and it tugs at my heart. I vow then and there to get my daughter back by whatever means necessary, because there's no way I'm letting them keep Lorelei knowing what they plan to do to her. Knowing what they allowed to happen to my mother.

"I'll get her back, I promise."

Although, I'm not ready to share my connection to the Sheridan Springs clan, I share part of my plan to get our daughter back. With Rylie onboard, it's time to tell the Westwood pack. Re-entering the cabin all eyes are on Rylie and me. I take the opportunity to scent the room, discovering something other than shifters. The aura of magic hovers in the air near the two women. Witches, I surmise, although one is more powerful than the other.

"Creed and I have decided it's best not to involve the Westwood pack."

Rylie says my name for the first time, and the sound of it on her lips hardens my cock at the most inopportune moment.

"I'm not a member of the pack," the older African American woman speaks up.

"But Santana is and he's your mate," Rylie replies.

"Do you know who took Lorelei?" Westwood asks.

Shaking my head, I provide the answer. "Not yet, but we have a place to start."

When it's clear to everyone I don't intend to elaborate, they appear to accept our decision. Everyone except the woman who appears to be like a mother to Rylie.

"If there's anything either of you need just ask," she pleas.

"We will," Rylie says, walking into the woman's embrace. "I promise."

Extending his hand to me, Westwood says. "Good luck to you both."

"Thank you," I reply, only to find myself extending my hand twice more to Westwood lookalikes and the younger witch who appears to be mated to one of the triplets.

One by one the Westwood pack offers well wishes, as they leave the cabin. Left alone with Rylie, I offer to take her home to pack a bag.

"I want to leave as soon as we can pack what we need for a few days and be on our way."

"The sooner we get started, the sooner we can get Lorelei back."

Leaving the cabin behind, we stop at Rylie's place first. I follow her direction to her small two-bedroom cottage that's not too far from the Westwood cabin.

"I'll only be a few minutes," Rylie says before hopping out of the truck.

Nodding, I accept that she doesn't intend to invite me into her home. And why would she when she sees me as nothing more than a stranger she shared her heat with a lifetime ago. Albeit a stranger she had a child with. I'm not even sure she feels this connection as deeply as I do considering she rejected me and kept my child from me.

Returning to my cabin to find Rylie gone from my bed three years ago devastated me. In a fit of rage over her rejection I allowed my bear to destroy the cabin. Regaining control took some effort, so when I managed to cage my bear again and repair the cabin, pride kept me from pursuing her.

Instead of searching for Rylie I put my tracking skills to use with the U.S. Marshals Service. Bear shifters are supernaturally dominant, large and powerful; therefore we're predisposed in many ways to be successful predators, which made apprehending wanted fugitives the perfect job for me.

Noticing the time, a few minutes has turned into nearly thirty, I decide to find out what's holding Rylie up. Why today of all days did she have to walk back into my life. With her mesmerizing blue eyes, golden blonde hair, and that luscious body I've craved continuously for three long years.

Once I decide I've waited long enough, I climb out of the Explorer onto a graveled path that leads to the front porch. Taking the steps two at a time, I tap my knuckles against the door. When she doesn't answer, I test the doorknob, thankfully it's unlocked. At first glance Rylie's home is just what a home should be, warm and inviting.

I take a few steps pass the front door when I hear Rylie's voice. Following the sound, I stop at her bedroom door finding it partially open. Unfortunately, the next words out of her mouth has my bear raging against his cage. Taking a step back, I retreat before I lose control.

"I love you too, Logan, my moonbeam, and when I get Lorelei back we'll be a family again."

Climbing back into my truck, I blast the radio loudly hoping the lyrics of the song will erase the words repeating on a loop in my head.

Chapter 5
Rylie

ENTERING MY BEDROOM, I pack what I need quickly, before the sight of the twin's unmade toddler beds stop me in my tracks. The urge to make their beds consume me until I give in to it. Picking up Lorelei's favorite teddy bear, I hold it to my nose breathing in the scent of my little girl. After I've made the beds, I call Naomi, defying CPS's no contact rule. The line rings twice before she answers without preamble.

"Are you okay?"

"I'm falling apart, Naomi. I'm desperate to find Lorelei, but I can't leave without speaking to my son. I need to hear Logan's voice before I go."

"I understand," she says before I hear her calling out to Logan. "Come here, cuddle bear, I have a surprise for you."

"Hello."

Hearing my son's voice, tears begin to stream down my cheeks, and I want so badly to go to him, to see him before I leave.

"Hello, Moonbeam."

"Mommy!"

"Yes, my moonbeam, it's mommy."

"I thought the bad monster hurt you."

"No baby, mommy's okay."

"But he took Lori."

"I know, but I'm going to go get her back. And while I'm gone I want you to be a good boy for Omi and Santa, okay."

"Okay, mommy, I love you."

"I love you too, Logan, my moonbeam, and when I get Lorelei back we'll be a family again."

Ending the call, I wipe my tears away before stuffing Lorelei's teddy bear into my bag. I make my way pass the living room to the front porch. Once outside the music from Creed's truck is loud enough to be annoying. Ignoring it for now, I lock the door before returning to the vehicle to face the man and his extremely loud music.

When I open the passenger door, Creed's head snaps my way as if I'd startled him, but the look in his heated stare screams anger not fear.

"I'm ready when you are." I say, turning the radio down and buckling my seat belt.

The engine revs as Creed pulls out my driveway. I assume he's demonstrating his obvious objection to me touching his radio. With less than nothing to say, I ignore his attitude. My only concern is Lorelei. This big bear of a man can stay grumpy for all I care as long as he helps me get my little girl back.

Creed's home turns out to be a cabin at Westwood Inn. Parking directly in front of the cabin, he climbs out with not so much as a, *wait here*. When he returns a few minutes later carrying a large black duffle bag I recognize from three years ago, the memory of wearing his blue flannel shirt comes unbidden, and that's when I realize he's no longer wearing his sheriff's uniform. He's dressed casually in a pair of dark blue jeans and a lighter blue button-down denim shirt. Although he's strikingly handsome in his uniform, the change of clothing has me eager to see what's underneath.

With his Stetson blocking his eyes from the sun and his head slightly bowed it's hard to read his expression. However, when he opens the backseat passenger door and grabs my bag his instructions are clear. I'm to follow him.

Following Creed gives me a spectator's view of his muscular backside. As we approach a midnight black Chevy Silverado 1500 , the alarm system chirps letting me know the doors have unlocked. From the driver's side Creed opens the back passenger door, tossing our bags inside. Since I'm not expecting him to open the door for me, I climb into the front passenger seat, shut the door and secure my seat belt.

Behind the wheel of his massive truck, Creed starts the engine and I swear my stomach roared much louder. Turning to face me he doesn't attempt to hide the frown on his face.

Embarrassed, I confess. "It's dinner time and I haven't eaten since breakfast."

"We'll stop for a bite to eat and fuel up before we get started," he says curtly.

"I thought we could stop at a drive-thru on the way, since the shifter who kidnapped Lorelei has put hundreds of miles between us already."

"There isn't a drive-thru for more than a hundred miles and my truck needs gas."

Protesting, I lie. "I can wait."

"Have you ever driven nearly seven hundred miles with a hungry bear?"

"You said the nearest drive-thru is one hundred miles."

"It is, but if you refuse to eat when you need to it may as well be. So we're having dinner now and fueling up before we hit the road."

"Fine," I pout.

Leaving Westwood Inn behind we stop at Santana's for dinner. As Creed dines on steak and potatoes, I feast on the house special, a large bowl of chili with all the toppings and a piece of warm cornbread. We didn't waste time talking during dinner, our minds seem to be elsewhere. Mine set on finding Lorelei and getting back home to Logan. The gods only knows what keeps that stoney expression on Creed's face.

Within an hour we hit the road heading to Sheridan Springs, Utah, my home town and the home of the Sheridan Springs bear shifters. A quiet drive with scenic views should be relaxing, unfortunately for me it's anything but. Breaking the ice barrier that's seems to have form between myself and Creed, I attempt small talk. I may as well get to know the father of my children.

"Thank you for agreeing to help get my daughter back."

"Our daughter," Creed corrects.

"Yes, of course she's our daughter."

"Then why did you keep her away from me?"

I know I should've prepared myself better for his question, but I didn't. Even if I had another three years to do so I still wouldn't be able to fully explain all the reasons I ran from him or why I never tried to find him.

"I needed to see what I could become on my own, away from my clan."

"I'm not a part of your clan, but you chose to run away from me anyway."

"How can I make you understand that I wasn't actually running away from you. I was running towards me."

"You can't"

Turning up the radio, Creed effectively ends our conversation. So, I take his not-so-subtle hint. Retrieving my cell phone from my pocket, I plug in my EarPods and watch the video of Lorelei and Logan on the day of our picnic at Westwood Falls splashing each other in the water.

• • • •

I DON'T KNOW HOW LONG I slept, but when I awake we're less than a mile from the Utah state line driving through a heavy rain storm. Even with the windshield wipers working overtime, it's still difficult to see the road directly in front of us. Reaching for Creed, I gasp loudly when he barely dodges an uprooted tree in the middle of the road.

"There," I say, pointing to a red neon light that reads, MO EL. "I assume that's a motel. We can't get Lorelei back if we're dead."

Forced to seek shelter we pull into the parking lot of the motel.

"Stay here," he says, hopping out of the safety of the vehicle into the heavy downpour of rain and strong winds mother nature has unleashed on the residents of Mesa.

When the darken night sky along with the heavy rain prevents me from seeing out the window of the truck clearly, I nearly jump out of my skin when Creed opens the passenger door startling me.

"Oh my gods," I shriek. "You scared the crap out of me."

"Let's go," he commands, extending his hand.

The instant I accept Creed's offered hand it felt like what being struck by lightning might feel like. A jolt of electrifying heat began to flow through my veins sending a warm current throughout my body targeting the essence of my core. I meet his gaze and it takes me a moment to realize I'm staring when the look in his eyes says he felt it too.

"I can manage," I insist, pulling my hand away.

Stepping out of the truck on shaky legs, I manage to follow Creed to the motel room. At first glance the room appears clean, but it has only one bed. Abruptly, I turn to Creed hoping he's just escorting me to my room.

Answering my unspoken question, he says. "This is the only room available."

"Of course it is," I murmur. "As if this day couldn't get any worse."

Creed huffs then stalks out the door only to return moments later with our bags.

"You can't seriously be considering staying here with me?" I ask.

Tossing the bags on the floor, Creed removes his soaked shirt. "As I said this is the only room available."

Staring at his bare chest, I forget my manners.

"Your virtue is safe with me; I'll sleep on the floor," he says.

I know I'm not being fair; he needs to rest as much as I do. Feeling a little ashamed, I lower my head in an attempt to hide my face when guilt pricks at my conscious. I'd swear my bear chuckles when I tell myself I can handle lying in a bed next to Creed for one night.

"It's a large bed, I'm sure there's enough room for both of us," I concede.

As tired as I am, I'm sure I'll be fast asleep in no time. Creed and I won't be repeating history tonight.

Creed groans, and I feel it in my core. "I need a shower," he says, before lifting his duffle bag from the floor.

Nodding, I try not to imagine his gorgeous naked body lathered in soap. I had to forget how his wet body feels against mine. Since my time in Creed's cabin I haven't allowed anyone to see or touch my body, and honestly I haven't wanted anyone in that way, human or shifter. After sharing so much with Creed in such a short span of time, I've been irrevocably changed by it.

There's no way anyone will ever compare to Creed. He was my first kiss, and he shared my first heat. Although we're fated mates, I don't bare his mark. Now I fear since we haven't consummated our bond it may be too late.

I force myself not to think about what will happen to me and Lorelei once I return to Sheridan Springs. I know what happens when omegas breed outside their clan. They are forced to abort the cub, forced to become a breeder for the clan. Not to mention they can never be claimed as a mate. The bathroom door creeks open, and I put away my worst fears.

Creed enters the bedroom freshly showered with a towel hanging low on his hips, and gods help me I can't resist the urge to sneak a look down at his impressive cock hanging long on his thigh. A soft moan escapes my lips, and I know I'm in deep trouble.

Lifting my eyes to his face, I'm pleased to see his ever-present frown seems to have disappeared. Seeing him clearly, I wonder what has changed his demeanor in just a few minutes. Unfortunately, now isn't the time to get lost in Creed Masterson when my own wet clothes cling to me like a second skin.

"The shower is all yours," he says smirking."

"Thank you."

Noticing him staring at my wet T-shirt, I scurry from the room.

"I thought we were being fair," he says, and the sound of his chuckle reach me behind closed doors.

Locked inside the bathroom, I strip off my wet clothing, only to realize I forgot to grab my bag in my haste to avoid Creed's scrutinizing gaze. Spying his open duffle bag, I grab the T-shirt on top before stepping under the hot spray of the shower.

As some of the tension begins to leave my body, the water turns cold. I grab the remaining unused towel and dry off quickly before pulling Creed's massive T-shirt over my head.

"Feel better?" He asks without looking up from his laptop.

"Much."

"What can you tell me about the shifter who took Lorelei."

"That's the first time you've said her name."

Looking up from his laptop, Creed's gaze roam my body approvingly, and the heated look in his eyes warms me all over.

"You're wearing my shirt." He practically growls and my bear inch closer to the surface

"I hope you don't mind that I borrowed it?"

He said nothing for long seconds, so I sat down on the bed beside him. Inhaling Creed's masculine scent, a combination of male shifter and Juniper has my body leaning toward his enticing scent of its own volition wanting desperately to be covered in it.

"She's my daughter and it's a lovely name," he finally says.

"It was my mother's name. She passed away giving birth to me."

"I'm sorry that you never got to know your mother."

"And I'm sorry I didn't give you a chance to know your daughter."

"No one is going to stop me from getting her back."

Remembering that I have additional information that could help, I retrieve my cell phone from the bedside table.

"I had lunch with my father in Chesterfield Saturday, as I was leaving the diner I noticed a black pickup truck following me. I managed to get the license plate."

"That's a great place to start."

"I'm sure the driver is the same shifter that took Lorelei. He was also driving a black pickup truck with Utah plates.

Watching Creed tap the keys of his laptop, I smile when I see his focused expression mirrors the same one the twins make when they're concentrating.

"What's the license plate number?"

"It's Utah plate B674TP."

Creed enter the license as I call it out to him, frowning he says, "Is this the guy that took Lorelei?"

Peering over Creed's shoulder, I saw the face of the shifter that attack me and kidnapped my daughter. Rage simmers my blood, and before I realize it's happening, my claws extend ripping through the bedcover. A strong hand covers mine, soothing my bear, urging her to retreat.

"That's him." Hearing the growl of my bear lingering in my voice, I close my eyes and take a deep cleansing breath. Replacing the image of the shifter I want to murder with my bare hands, I focus on an image of Lorelei's smile.

"Yes, that's him. He's the shifter that took our daughter."

"He's a mercenary with no ties to any clan. He has many aliases, but the one he uses most often is Stryker."

"He came after me, not Lorelei. I remember him saying, "*You belong with a clan, omega,*"

"So why take Lorelei?"

"He heard her call me mommy, then he said something about a two for one omega special."

"Is it possible that someone from the Sheridan Springs clan could have hired him to bring you back?"

"Yes, it's possible. I was the last omega born to the clan as far as I know."

"That's unusual isn't it."

"I guess it depends on the clan. The Council of Elders of the Sheridan Springs clan has been forcing alpha-omega unions for nearly one hundred years. Without the alpha-omega union the magic of the clan begins to die. That's why the Council of Elders instituted the breeding law for omegas and created the alpha challenge to create new alphas when necessary. It ensures the shifter magic of the clan continues. If my father had a son, his reign as alpha wouldn't have been challenged and I wouldn't have been subjected to the breeding law."

"My father's clan is very different. Omegas aren't treated as possession. They're honored and cherished. And when it comes to choosing a mate, she's free to have more than one if she desires it, unless she finds her fated mate."

"I can't imagine ever wanting multiple mates."

"Neither can I."

"Your father's clan sounds like a save place for omegas."

"It wasn't always," Creed murmurs, but I hear it clearly. "Knowing who we're looking for is a great place to start once we reach Sheridan Springs," he says closing his laptop.

"We should get some sleep before heading out again," I suggest.

"Goodnight, Rylie."

"Goodnight, Creed."

Climbing into bed, I pull the bedcover up over my shoulders, as the room falls into darkness. After turning off the lights Creed sinks into the bed on the opposite side, lying atop the bedcover. I don't know how long I lie perfectly still pretending to be asleep before sleep actually claims me. What I do know is that my body overheating wakes me before sunrise. Creed's heady scent wraps me in a calm familiar bubble I've only ever experienced with him. Even my bear likes how it feels mentally cuddling in his arms. Knowing my bear recognizes Creed as my fated mate has me settling back into a peaceful slumber.

Chapter 6
Creed

WAKING WITH MY FATED mate's body nestled against mine has my cock throbbing achingly with need. I don't know when it happened but at some point Rylie managed to cuddle up next to me. Her head resting on my chest satisfies my inner bear's need to protect her. I must admit I love how the soft curves of her body fits perfectly against the hard arches of mine. Daring to take what I need; I press my lips against Rylie's for a brief kiss. It's not as satisfying as our first kiss, but it sates my hunger for now.

Rolling Rylie from my arms so as not to wake her, I'm unprepared for her reaction. With her fist clutching my T-shirt tightly, I'm encouraged to stay put. So, I do. Sleepily she snuggles closer, and I nearly lose my fucking mind when her leg crosses mine exposing her bare pussy to my thigh. My cock hardens in response which is no surprise. I've wanted my mate every day since the moment I knew she was meant for me.

I fight the urge to touch her, however, when needful moans escape her lips and her gentle breath caress my neck, I lose it. Sliding my hand under the T-shirt she borrowed for me, I find her tender bud easily. With a few teasing strokes, Rylie's moans become louder as her hips chase my fingers seeking pleasure.

"Please," she whispers, and I rejoice knowing she's fully awake.

"Are you sure, Goldie?" Staring up at me, Rylie seems to have second thoughts. So, I ask again. "Is this what you want,

Rylie?" I punctuate each word with a stroke against her throbbing little nub.

"Yes, Creed. Please don't stop."

I forget about this Logan character my mate and my daughter have made a family with and I concentrate on the fact that Rylie wants me now. I focus on what I know for certain, I know how to pleasure her, and I know how to make her scream my name.

My lips descend upon hers as my middle finger part her folds before sinking into her needy wet heat. Her breath quickens, the seductive sound music to my ears. Adding another finger, I sink them deep into her tight warm core. The smell of her desire is a heady scent, a potent aphrodisiac to my bear. Breathing in the scent of her arousal has me dying to taste her again.

Pulling away, I meet her gaze. "I need to see you, Goldie, all of you," I groan.

Nodding, Rylie gives her consent for me to strip her bare. I tug at the hem of the T-shirt, lifting it over her head before tossing it aside. Spreading her thighs wide, I lay between them, and with one hand I pin her hands above her head. I watch as her nipples harden unable to resist a taste. Capturing her right breast in the grip of my hand, I praise it with attention. Licking, sucking, and biting her nipple has her writhing beneath me. My lips mark a blazing trail down her body. I stop to admire her flat belly, striated with fine stretch marks she no doubt received after giving birth to our daughter.

"These are beautiful," I say kissing her stomach.

Blushing, Rylie tries to look away.

"Eyes on me, Rylie Adams, watch me admire this beautiful body of yours."

The lower my lips travel down the length of my mate's body, the scent of her arousal fills my nostrils causing my cock to swell and press painfully into the mattress. With Rylie laid out for me like an all you can eat buffet; I indulge my hunger for her. My tongue sinks between her glistening folds, and the first taste of her sweet nectar in three years has my cock throbbing violently with envy.

Rylie's moans of pleasure wakes the quiet room, filling it with whispered curses and soft pleas for more. I desperately want to give her what she needs, but not yet.

A hard suck to Rylie's swollen throbbing bundle of nerves has her pulling at my hair holding me against her needy wet pussy. Grinding against my mouth, her back arches off the bed, reaching for the orgasm I've denied her until now. Until I hear her say the one word I've waited to hear since we triggered the mate bond.

"Creed!"

"Say it again, Rylie. Scream my name." Sinking three fingers into the depths of her warm inviting pussy, I pump and suck until she explodes on my tongue.

"Yes! Creed! Yes!"

Lapping and sucking Rylie's essence until her body goes lax and her moans gives way to gentle whimpers, my bear growls his approval.

Mine. He says, settling into his cage.

Freeing Rylie for my hold, I allow her a few moments to recover before we need to hit the road again. I make my way to the bathroom to take a piss and clean up a bit before getting dressed. It takes me all of five minutes to return to the bedroom where I find Rylie still lying spread eagle atop the bedcover. Normally such an enticing view of my mate would be too tempting to resist. But not today when I have to find the motherfucker who kidnapped my daughter and make him regret ever laying eyes on her.

"Rise and shine, Goldie. It's time to get going."

"Two more minutes," she pleas, hiding her face under the bedcover.

"We don't have two minutes; our daughter needs us to find her."

Sitting up abruptly in bed, Rylie exclaims. "Shit! I can't believe I let an orgasm zap my memory."

Rylie seems to have forgotten her shyness as she climbs out of bed naked. I watch her rifle through her bag for a change of clothing before pulling out a tan lace trim bra with matching panties, a black T-shirt and dark wash jeans. With her clothes in hand she grabs her toiletry bag before striding to the bathroom. The gentle sway of her hips seduces me with every step she takes.

I gather our things, preparing to leave when I spy a stuff teddy bear poking out of Rylie's bag. Realizing it must belong to our daughter, Lorelei, I pull the stuff bear free from the bag and lift it up to my nose. My heart skips a beat, recognizing my blood, Rylie's blood in our daughter's scent. It's all there. More determined than ever to find her, I memorize her scent.

Stuffing the teddy bear back into Rylie's bag, I lift it onto the bed for her to finish packing away her things. It takes my mate ten minutes to step out of the bathroom completely refreshed. Slipping her bare feet into a pair of black Converse sneakers she appears ready to go.

"All set," she says, shoving her toiletry bag into her overnight bag, before lifting it from the bed.

"Taking the bag from her, I reply, "Now you are."

I step out into the morning air with Rylie at my side. At first glance other than an excess amount of leaves and debris on the ground, the storm didn't leave any lasting damage.

"Where's the key?" Rylie asks as we approach my Silverado.

"My right front pocket."

Intending to retrieve the key myself, Rylie beats me to it. By reaching into my pocket first she manages to retrieve my key while simultaneously giving me a raging hardon. I swear this woman is purposely giving me blue balls.

"I hope I didn't overstep."

"Goldie, I just had my tongue and fingers deep in the sweet heat between your thighs. So, I'm good with you grabbing a key for my pocket."

Blushing, she lowers her gaze to my very obvious erection. "But I shouldn't have done that."

"It was done the moment I woke and found you in my arms."

"But you didn't..."

The sight of Rylie blushing is quickly becoming my favorite new obsession.

"I didn't what, Goldie."

"You didn't finish. I mean we didn't have sex."

Lifting Rylie's chin so her eyes meet mine, I say. "We didn't have time. But just so you know, the next time you offer yourself to me, I'm taking everything."

Rylie's bear makes her presence known, enthralling me as my mate's normally vibrant blue eyes turn a deep chocolate brown.

"Your bear approves," I say, planting a chaste kiss on her lips.

Batting her lashes, Rylie unlocks my truck before climbing into the passenger seat. I toss our bags into the back seat and a feeling a certainty overcomes me. I join Rylie, taking my place in the driver's seat committed to winning my mate's heart.

• • • •

AFTER DRIVING NEARLY three hours we finally reach Sheridan Springs. Knowing we'll likely be here for a couple of days; I pull into the Sheridan Springs Inn.

"I hope you've gotten over your objections to sharing a room with me. Because now that we're here I'm not letting you out of my sight."

"I can stay with my father."

"I'm not letting you out of my sight," I repeat.

"It's probably for the best anyway. There's still a lot I haven't told him."

"He doesn't know you had a child?" I ask, making a discerning guess.

Shaking her head, Rylie confesses. "He's only been back in my life for six months, and I wanted to be sure he wouldn't inform the Council of Elders."

''I'm sure he'll understand your need to protect your child. Any parent would."

"I hope so."

"After we check into the hotel, we'll pay your father a visit."

The former alpha may have some insight into what the council and current alpha are up to regarding my mate and daughter.

"Sounds good," Rylie agrees.

At the front desk, the hotel clerk attempts to observe Rylie inconspicuously. Unfortunately, for her my observation skills are much sharper.

"How long will you be staying, Mr. Masterson?" She asked swiping my credit card for the room.

"No longer than we need to," I reply, accepting the room's key card along with the return of my credit card.

"Well I hope you enjoy your stay at Sheridan Springs Inn, however long you decide to stay."

Nodding my thanks, I escort Rylie to the elevator, and we ride three floors up in silence to locate room 325. With my hands full, Rylie inserts the key card to unlock the door. Entering first, I drop our bags near the door to inspect the room for any unwelcomed guest.

"All clear?" Rylie asks once my inspection is complete.

"All clear," I confirm.

"I think the clerk at the front desk recognized me."

"It's possible but were not hiding. If someone comes for you they'll have to get through me first."

Looking up at me, Rylie smiles. "I've never met a bear shifter as large as you. How big are you?"

Smirking, I tease, "I'm just the right size for you, Goldie."

"I meant how big is your bear?" She blushes sweetly.

"My bear is a Kodiak, so pretty damn big."

"Really!" She shrieks. "Most of the shifters I've seen are Grizzlys, but some are smaller than others."

"My mother was a Grizzly, but my father was a Kodiak."

"Was?" Rylie questions.

"They're both deceased."

"I'm so sorry for your loss, Creed."

"It was a longtime ago."

"The amount of time doesn't matter; I can tell you still miss them. My mother died giving birth to me, but I still miss her even though I've never met her."

"My father died when I was just a cub, and my mother essentially died slowly of a broken heart."

"They were fated mates."

"They were."

Without meaning to I allow a cloud of grief to envelop me, rendering me speechless for long seconds.

"We don't have to talk about them if it upsets you, but I would love to know more about your parents."

"Maybe some other time."

"Sure."

Moving on pass my somber mood, I ask. "And what about your bear, what is she?"

"She's a blonde Grizzly."

Of their own volition my feet move in Rylie's direction, stopping directly in front of her. Lifting Rylie's hair from her shoulder, I allow her silky golden blonde strands to glide through my fingers.

"I've never felt anything so soft."

"I'm told my mother was a natural blonde, although her bear was brown."

"What color is our daughter's hair?"

"Blonde. She's my mini-me, she even has the same blue eyes as me. She has your smile, and she's bossy for an omega. So I'm guessing that's all you."

"Or she's an alpha."

"There's never been a female alpha in the Sheridan Springs clan."

"That doesn't mean she won't be the first."

"As long as she as the freedom to choose her own destiny, I'll be a proud mamma bear."

Releasing Rylie's hair, I ask the question that has been bothering me since seeing my mate again.

"Is that why you rejected me after our mate bond triggered. You wanted the freedom to choose your own destiny?"

Putting some distance between us, Rylie takes a seat on the edge of the bed. I can practically see her mind working to find the right words to say. One day she'll realize that I prefer not to have a sugar-coated version of the truth.

"Just speak your truth, Rylie. I can handle it."

"We spent nearly forty-eight hours in bed satisfying my heat, and in my lust fevered mind I never wanted to leave you. However, when my heat gave way to clearer thinking, I knew I couldn't stay no matter how much I wanted to. I'd shamed my father by running away, forcing him to forfeit his right to be alpha. I felt guilty for all I'd done in the name of freedom. I didn't even know what I wanted from life, but there I was already mated to a man I'd just met. So I ran until I discovered I was pregnant a few days later."

"Is that how you ended up in Westwood?"

"Yes, it was purely dumb luck. I was hiding out in the forest near the cottage I now call home when the owner spotted me.

She invited me in, cleaned me up, fed me, and gave me a place to stay while I was pregnant."

"Let me guess, the owner is the older woman I saw at Westwood's cabin."

"Yes, her name is Naomi Morgan."

"She seems very protective."

"She is. I'm lucky to have her as a friend."

"I need you to know I intend to do everything in my considerable power to get our daughter back and claim you as my fated mate so that we can me a family."

"I..."

Interrupting her, I add. "Without realizing it, I've waited for you to walk back into my life again. Now that you have, I know what it feels like to have a connection with someone that's so deep no amount of time or distance will ever sever it. We're fated, my mate, and I'll wait for you to accept the truth about us."

Tugging Rylie up from her seat on the bed, I announce, "It's time I met your father."

Chapter 7
Rylie

THE RIDE TO MY FATHER'S to pay him an unexpected visit with my fated mate in tow, is necessary to find our daughter. However, Creed confessing his intentions has my mind totally blown. I never would have believed he wanted us as a family until he said the words. Until this morning, all I felt from him was cold distance and animosity.

I'm not sure how to take the sudden change. I want to believe him, but what do I truly know about him. I know he lost both his parents, and his bear is a big ass Kodiak and he's my fated mate. With his last words still echoing in my head, I find it hard to ignore our connection. However, fated mate or not, it's time we bare ourselves to each other. I wonder how he'll take having two cubs instead of just one, a son and a daughter.

Pulling into my father's drive way, I wish I could say it evokes fond memories of me and my friends hanging out in the front yard. Instead it only serves to remind me of how isolated I felt growing up in this house.

Creed brings his Silverado to a stop behind my father's older Chevy pickup that's seen better days.

"Can we assume he's home?" Creed asks, removing the key from the ignition.

"He's home."

Climbing out of the truck, I take a few tentative steps toward the front porch before coming to an abrupt stop.

"I have to tell you something before we speak to my father."

"What is it, Goldie."

My father's booming voice reach my ears as I'm about to tell Creed about Logan.

"By the gods, Rylie is that truly you?" My father asks, bounding down the steps two at a time.

Scooping me up in his arms, hugging me tightly is a welcome surprise considering the distance I felt growing between us after our lunch date a few days ago. When he finally notice Creed walking up behind me, he places me firmly on my feet. Not realizing that Creed's with me my father asks.

"What can I do for you?"

"It's a pleasure to meet you, sir. I'm Creed Masterson, your daughter's fated mate."

Snapping my gaze back to Creed, I almost miss my father's expression of approval. Scenting the air my father gives both Creed and I a questioning look.

"If she's your fated mate why haven't you claimed her as yours."

"That's a bit more complicated," Creed replies.

"Why don't you both come inside, and we'll see if we can uncomplicate it."

"Lead the way," Creed says, taking my hand in his.

It's been a long time since I step foot in my father's house, and returning unsettles me more than I care to admit. Following him into the family room, I watch him take a seat in his favorite recliner opposite his large flat screen television. With my hand held possessively in Creed's we take a seat on the couch opposite my father.

"Now tell me why claiming my daughter as your fated mate is complicated," my father says, picking up where he left off.

"Before we get into that, I need your help." Amending my request, I add. "We need your help, father."

Hearing the urgency in my tone, my father drags his attention away from Creed to focus on me.

"Whatever you need," he says, reaching out to take my free hand.

"Our daughter has been kidnapped."

In a matter of seconds my father's expression goes from shock to anger to joy before settling somewhere between hurt and disappointment.

"You had a child, and you didn't tell me I'm a grandfather not once in the last six months since we've been meeting for lunch. Why, Rylie? Why didn't you tell me?"

Tears well in my eyes, witnessing my father's heartbreak.

"I had to know I could trust you. I couldn't risk the Council of Elders finding us."

"Do you even live in Chesterfield?" My father asks, releasing my hand as if the physical contact offends him.

Shaking my head, I murmur, "No, Westwood."

Before my father voices another word, Creed comes to my defense.

"Sir, try to understand Rylie's point of view. What she did she did to protect our daughter, not to deprive you of your grandchild."

The room falls silent and for a moment my father appears to be considering Creed's words.

"And yet it doesn't change the fact that her actions robbed me of everything. My chance at remaining alpha, my daughter and now apparently my granddaughter."

Tugging my hand free of Creed's grasp, I kneel at my father's feet. "I never meant to shame you father, I never meant to hurt you, please forgive me." I beg.

As if the sight of me on my knees begging for forgiveness triggers something in Creed, he stands, and in one fluid motion pulls me up on my feet, turning me to face him.

"Don't ever apologize for doing what's best for you or our child. Any good parent will do whatever it takes to protect their child," Creed says, wiping my tears away before placing a tender kiss on my forehead.

Turning to face my father, I feel confident in Creed's arms. "I can't change what I've done, and it was never my intention to shame or hurt you, so I hope you can find it in your heart to forgive me someday, but for now will you help us find our daughter."

Standing, my father towers over me, forcing me to tilt my head to meet the piercing gaze of his hazel eyes.

"Of course I'll do what I can to bring my granddaughter home safely." Creed extends his hand to my father, and he accepts. "Tell me what you know." My father says, releasing Creed's hand.

After we've taken our seats again, I start by telling my father about the bear shifter that came for me but took Lorelei instead after he attacked me and left me bleeding out. Hearing me recount the details that led to our daughters kidnapping, Creed unleashes a menacing growl and the eyes of his bear surfaces making his presence known. Trapped between two bear shifters with one on the brink of losing control, I do what I can to calm them.

Squeezing my father's hand I attempt to reassure him. "I'm okay," I add before quickly releasing his hand to turn my attention to my mate.

"Creed," I soothe, hoping my voice will calm his bear. "I need you to cage your Kodiak." I press my lips to Creed's, waiting for his snarl to give way to the pressure of my kiss. Aware that my father has left us alone in the family room, I slide onto Creed's lap, straddling him. "I'm here and I'm okay," I whisper the words against his lips.

"Goldie," he growls, slipping his tongue into my mouth and shoving his hands into my hair.

Our kiss has gone from coaxing to desperate need when Creed's hardening cock throbs against my center. Unable to contain the rush of heat flowing directly to my core, I grind against the big bulge in his pants. Breaking our kiss, I meet his gaze, and it's filled with the same intense desire I feel.

My gasps and moans grow louder when Creed's hands slip under my T-shirt. The claws of his bear cups my breast before pulling my bra down under them. I watch in awe as my mate press my breast together before lowering his head and sucking both of my harden nipples into his mouth at the same time. I nearly lose my fucking mind, as indescribable pleasure races to my core. I ride the imprint of his cock, chasing my release, never taking my eyes off him.

I don't know how long we stay entwined in each other's arms before I hear the sound of voices at the front door. With Creed's bear under control, I climb off his lap reluctantly, and do my best not to look like a woman who just had an amazing orgasm.

"We heard Rylie has returned." I hear a familiar voice say.

"And where did you hear that?" My father questions.

"You should know by now, Branson, the council has spies everywhere."

Creed stands, and together we join my father at the door.

Although my father hasn't invited the members of the Council of Elders into his home, I see the faces of Preema Ellis and Denna Miles clearly.

"Good to see you again." Denna smiles, seeing me approach with Creed at my side.

"Hello, Denna," I say, returning her greeting.

"We're here on behalf of the Council of Elders to formally request your attendance at a hearing for you to answer for your crimes against the clan's new alpha," Preema says without preamble.

"And if she declines your request?" Creed asks.

"If she refuses to honor the request, we'll be forced to escort her personally."

Creed steps forward and Preema takes a step back. "Touch my mate and you die." Creed threatens between clenched teeth.

"Your mate?" Denna asks, attempting to mask her surprised expression.

Sniffing the air, Preema says, "Yet she remains unclaimed."

"And my mate nonetheless."

Drawing Creed's attention away from Preema, I take his hand in mine, and urge him to step away from the much smaller female shifters.

"When and where is this hearing scheduled to take place?" I ask.

"Tomorrow 10:00 a.m." Denna provides. "At the town hall."

"I'll be there."

"We'll be there," Creed adds.

Nodding, Preema is the first to walk away, with Denna following close behind. My father, Creed and I remain standing at the front door, watching the familiar black jeep as it backs out of the driveway. Once the vehicle is out of sight, my father closes the door, and we return to the family room.

"We need to get back to finding Lorelei," I say ending the silence and breaking through some of the tension in the room.

"Lorelei? You named my granddaughter after your mother?" My father ask, as his lips curl up in an approving grin.

Deciding it's time to reveal my final secret, I ask Creed and my father to take a seat. Two sets of curious eyes stare at me, watching me pace the floor as I search for the right words.

"I'd hope to tell you this in private," I say, facing Creed.

"Tell me what?" He asks anxiously.

"Lorelei has a brother; his name is Logan."

"Two grandchildren." My father announces gleefully. "And you named them both after your mother."

Still facing Creed's silence, I nod, "My mother's given name was Lorelei Logan."

"Logan is your son?" He asks as if he's just realizing what I've said.

"Yes, Logan is our son," I correct. "Lorelei's twin brother."

Standing, Creed stalks towards me with an unreadable expression marring his handsome face. In a few quick strides he has me in his arms, twirling me around the room. The sound of his laughter fills my ears and warms my heart. I wrap my arms around his neck holding onto him tightly, never wanting to let him go.

"You're not angry with me for not telling you about Logan right away?"

"I heard you on the phone with him, and I thought..."

"What did you think?" I ask when Creed goes quiet before finishing his sentence.

"It doesn't matter," he assures me with a chaste kiss.

Placing me firmly on my feet, Creed turns to face my father.

"I have a son, sir." Creed announces proudly.

"Congratulations, my boy. Now let's find your daughter so you both can get back home to your son."

Over the next few hours Creed tracks Stryker's movements using the license plate I gave him via traffic cameras from Westwood to Timber Valley where he seems to fall off the map.

"I'll reach out to my father's clan for help tracking Stryker. And after the hearing we'll leave for Timber Valley."

Understanding there's nothing more we can do until we find Stryker, I lead Creed to my father's kitchen. We join my father at the large circular dining table, and the three of us enjoy a quiet home cooked meal together.

After dinner, my father clears the table, but I insist on washing the dishes. Pulling my iPhone from my back pocket, I ask, "Would either of you like to see photos of the twins?"

"Yes." They say in unison.

Handing my phone over to Creed, I watch the two enormous bear shifters hover over the small screen viewing photos of the twins with bright smiles spreading across their faces. I turn back to the task at hand, packing up leftovers before washing the dishes.

"Do you mind if I send myself the photos?" Creed asks.

"I have hundreds of photos, send as many as you like."

"I'll text a few to my phone now, but I intend to download the rest to my laptop later," Creed says, meeting my gaze.

I feel my core spasm rapidly under his intense scrutiny. My feet move of their own volition moving towards my mate.

"Send as many as you can my way," my father adds.

"Help yourself," Creed says, passing my phone over to my father.

Taking me by the hand, he leads me back to the family room. I follow him obediently, eager for a moment alone with him.

"You've given me two precious gifts," Creed whispers as he pins me to the nearest wall.

I hear the back door open and close, sure that my father has stepped outside to give us a little privacy. Unfortunately, with his shifter hearing the gesture may be for nothing.

"I believe my father approves of our mate bond," I breathe against his lips.

A broad smile spreads across Creed's lips before he murmurs against mine. "I only care if I'm who you want. No one else's opinion matters to me."

"I've never stop wanting you, Creed. Can't you tell?" I whisper the truth for his ears only. "My body yearns to have you inside me again."

"I can smell your arousal, and I can't deny how your body responds to my touch, but I need to hear you say the words."

"Claim me, Creed. Accept me as your fated mate because I have no doubt that you are mine."

"Not here," he groans against my neck. "Not in your father's house and absolutely not against a wall. At least not until after I've claimed you fully for the first time.

"We should say goodnight to my father."

Leading me out the front door, Creed and I find my father sitting in his truck listening to his favorite radio station. When he see us approaching, he climbs out of the truck greeting us with a smile I haven't seen in a long time. A smile that reaches his eyes and lights up his soul. Creed releases my hand and I go to my father, hugging him tightly.

"Will you meet us at the town hall tomorrow for the hearing?" I ask.

"Don't you worry, sweetheart, I'll be there." Extending his hand to Creed, he says. "Your mate and I won't let you face the council alone."

"Goodnight, sir. We'll see you tomorrow morning,"

"I believe my daughter's fated mate has earned the right to call me Branson or Bran."

Dropping the formality, Creed replies, "We'll see you tomorrow, Branson."

My father returns my phone to me before planting a tender kiss on my forehead. From the front passenger seat of Creed's Silverado, I wave goodbye as the truck leaves the driveway. Seeing the figure of my father get smaller with distance, I'm hit with a powerful feeling of regret over the time I've lost with him. As tears cloud my vision the realization that the time I've stolen from my cubs with their own father can never be regained, an overwhelming tide of guilt batters my heart.

Chapter 8
Creed

BEFORE ENTERING THE hotel room with my mate's hand clasp securely in mine, I take a moment to allow my heighten sense of hearing and smell to determine the room is as we left it. Pleased to find no one had invaded our space, and eager to share my discovery with her, I lead Rylie inside.

Locking the door behind us, I turn to face my mate. That's when I notice Rylie's mood has changed. All the joy and heat I felt radiating off her has given way to a bout of melancholy. My need to keep her safe forces my protective instincts into high gear, as I push aside my need to possess her.

"Tell me what's upsetting you, Rylie."

"I'm not..."

"I can see it in your eyes," I interrupt. "So, don't deny your feelings, and don't deny me an honest answer."

Nodding, Rylie lowers her head as tears roll down her cheeks. Patiently, I wait until she's ready to speak. I know from experience how difficult it can be exposing the source of your pain. How difficult it can be to trust someone with that pain.

"I don't deserve your forgiveness. The time I stole from you and our cubs can never be recaptured. And it breaks my heart that I selfishly chose not to share them with you."

Unable to resist the pull of our mate bond, I scoop Rylie up into my arms. A few long quick strides carry us to our unused bed. With Rylie press snuggly to my chest, somehow I manage to toe my boots off before climbing onto the bed and rest my back against the headboard.

"I didn't lie when I told your father you did what any good parent would do to protect their child. You feared for your safety and the safety of our cubs. Don't ever apologize or ask forgiveness for doing what's best for you or our children."

Lifting Rylie's chin, I wipe away her tears when her eyes meet mine. Once I'm satisfied she sees the truth of my words in the depths of my eyes, my lips claim hers. Teasingly, I coax the heat of her passion back to life. Desperate needful moans, escape her throat only to be captured by mine.

"Do you have any idea what you do to me?"

"I have a pretty good idea," she whispers against my lips.

"I don't think you do."

Forcing myself to release my mate, I climb off the bed.

"Did I do something wrong?" She questions.

"Everything about you is just right for me, Goldie. So right in fact, it scares me shitless to think of a life without you and our cubs in it."

"How's it possible for a little grizzly to scare a massive Kodiak?" She teases, crawling on her hands and knees toward the foot of the bed where I stand cock hard, and frozen in place by the seduction of her movement.

I manage to shake my head, a feeble attempt to break the spell my mate has me under. Taking a few steps back, the distance seems to clear my head.

"You've been hiding who you are far too long, And before we go any further, I want you to know it's not too late to walk away."

"I don't understand, Creed. Are you saying you no longer want to claim me as your fated mate?"

"I'm giving you a choice while I still can."

"I've already made my choice; I want to consummate our mate bond."

"I want that too, more than anything."

"Then why are we still talking?"

"Because you're nearing your heat, and I won't claim what isn't mine."

Dumbfounded, Rylie's jaw gapes open as her eyes widen in shock. Her next words are a string of incoherent babbles. But I get the gist of what she's saying. She had been suppressing her heat since giving birth to the twins.

"I can scent your omega pheromones rising and my desire to rut grows with it."

"I barely missed a day. It shouldn't be returning this quickly. Should it?" She questions, and I hear the doubt in her voice.

"There's no way I'll ever forget your scent, Rylie. When I entered my cabin and found you, in full heat sleeping in my bed, your omega pheromones overwhelmed me. Even now I have to fight my body's natural response to claim my mate."

"I'm more than just an omega," she growls.

Hearing the angry bite of her words, my bear takes notice.

"Yes, you are, Goldie. You're brave, beautiful, kind, the mother of my cubs and my fated mate."

"Naomi once told me that the only thing strong enough to render her spell useless is accepting my fated mate. I've done that, and there's no going back, because I can no longer think of a life without you in it. I'm yours to claim, Creed."

Of their own volition my feet begin to move toward Rylie before guilt brings me to an abrupt halt. The voice I've come to recognize as my bear, chastises me for my lack of honesty with our mate. Unfortunately, instead of coming clean, I decide to tell a partial truth hoping to temper the sting of my rejection.

"I want you to know me, Rylie. But there are aspects of my life that I can't share with you right now, at least not until I've put the ghost of my past to rest."

"I'm not going anywhere, Creed. For now we can focus on getting our daughter back. There will be time for us later, after all our ghosts have been vanquished.

· · · ·

UNABLE TO FALL ASLEEP, I lie awake in bed with Rylie snugged safely in my arms. When sleep continues to elude me after several hours my mind begins rehashing recent events as if stuck on an endless loop. The sight of my fated mate kneeling and begging her father for forgiveness triggered a memory I'd been trying to forget for nearly thirty years.

I was barely five years old, when I witnessed my father's death at the hands of a bear shifter who coveted my mother, an omega for himself. The challenge was an easy win for my father. Unfortunately, the challenger didn't accept defeat with honor. I will never forget the sound of my mother's screams of warning to my father who had turned his back on his opponent. Shock and fear held me captive that day, as I watched in horror as the man shifted into a massive grizzly before pinning my father face down in the muck of the forest. His large paws pounded my father's back furiously, and his thick black claws mauled the flesh from his body. It wasn't until the beast rendered my father unconscious give way to the man once again. My father's blood saturated the hands of the shifter, dripping the crimson liquid onto the forest ground.

"Please don't kill him, he's my fated mate." My mother begged, dropping to her knees.

"Yet the Council of Elders promised you to me."

"Spare him, and I'll return to Sheridan Springs with you."

"Do you really think I want his sloppy seconds, or his brat of a cub as a constant reminder of your betrayal."

"I'll leave my son here with his father and I promise to never see them again."

"I'm no fool, omega. I won't risk your fated mate returning to claim you again someday."

"Please spare him, and I'll sever the mate bond. We can be mated."

"You're only good for breeding now, I'll never accept you as my mate. And since I can't have you as my mate, you won't have yours."

As a five-year-old I didn't understand, why the shifter had attacked my father after the challenge was over, or why my mother had promised to leave us. However, years later I grew to understand the vengeance that crept into my heart that day.

Now that both my parents are gone, my mother's dying words still echoes deep in my mind, reminding me to protect the ones most important to me.

Climbing out of bed, I do my best not to wake Rylie. After a bit of tossing and turning most of the night, she seems to be sleeping peacefully. Until her, it had never been difficult for me to leave a woman's bed. However, since reuniting with my fated mate, leaving her bed is the last thing I want to do. Ignoring the bulging hardon tenting my boxer briefs, and the scent of Rylie's heat rising to the surface, I make my way to the shower.

Alone under the rainfall of hot water, I fist my cock and allow my thoughts of Rylie's bare skin beneath me to keep me company. I imagine her warm wet heat sheathing me and I grow longer and thicker in my hand. As precum drips onto my fingers, my fist tightens around my shaft, and I stroke hard and fast, desperate for release.

When soft moans reach my ears, I turn to see Rylie watching me. Unashamed, I fuck my hand harder, silently daring my mate not to look away. Of its own volition my heartbeat syncs with Rylie's, and the rhythm of my strokes syncs with the ragged pants of her breath. The intense heat in her eyes tells me she needs this as much as I do, so I let go. Growling my release, my body shudders ejecting spurts of my seed onto the shower floor.

Without uttering a single word, Rylie strips off my oversized T-shirt, before joining me in the shower. Soft soapy hands glide over my shoulders and down my torso, bathing me as only a lover could. Although her touch keeps me perpetually hard and aching with need to claim her, I allow her hands to explore my body.

In a few days she'll be in full blown heat, triggering my need to rut, triggering our need to consummate the mate bond. Until then I will endure this pleasurable torture.

Chapter 9
Rylie

WAKING FROM A RESTLESS sleep, I'm not surprise to find I'm alone in bed. Although I understand why Creed wants to wait to claim me, we both have unresolved issues from our past hindering the path to our future together. I'm well aware that he has told me next to nothing about his life, and I'm okay with that for now. I also know the time will come when we will have to bare our bodies, minds and hearts to each other, as fated mates we won't be able to accept anything less than a soul deep bond.

When the chiming of my cell phone pulls my thoughts away from Creed, I retrieve the device from the bedside table, pleased to see a video message from Naomi. The moment Logan's face appears on the screen my heart skips a beat. And his bright smile tells me he's doing okay despite the trauma he experienced.

"Hi, mommy! I miss you! I love you!," he says excitedly.

"I love you too, moonbeam," I say to the video recording of my son.

Tears prick the corners of my eyes, when the sight of Logan appears atop a horse with Aria's mate Anakin. The two of them seem to be racing, Calian and his son Kota. The boys seem to be enjoying their playtime together, which makes me all the more grateful for Naomi and the Westwood pack. I don't know what I would have done if I had to worry about Logan's safety while searching for his sister.

When the video comes to an end, Naomi's face appears, and her words tug at my heart strings.

"I thought you might need a little something to brighten your day."

Sitting my phone aside, I scramble out of bed, ready to take on the Council of Elders before resuming my search for my daughter. Distracted by my thoughts, I enter the bathroom without knocking. And before I have time to back out, the sight of Creed pleasuring himself in the shower sends a fiery burst of heat to my core. I don't know how long I'm entranced by the flex of his bicep, the movement of his hand, and the size of his cock. But I'll never forget the look in his eyes when my mate catches me staring.

Unabashedly, Creed continues to stroke his cock, as if beckoning me to join him. My heart races with the possibility, my breath quickens with excitement, my core spasms with heat, but I stay rooted in place.

The sound of Creed's deep growl, followed by the spurt of his release wasted on the tile floor of the shower causes my core to ache enviously for his seed to fill me. Wordlessly, I undress before stepping into the shower. Eager to feel his glistening muscles beneath my fingertips, I lather his body with my soapy hands. My fingers trace the outline of his broad shoulders, dance over the peaks and valleys of his washboard abs, and cup his balls gently all under the guise of bathing my mate thoroughly.

"We can't stay in here forever, Goldie," Creed says, breaking the spell of our intimate bubble.

Forcing my fingers to stop their exploration, I agree.

"I know."

"Next time, I'll bathe you," he says with a cocky grin.

"Deal."

Stepping out of the shower, Creed takes me by the hand urging me to follow. With no time to waste we dry ourselves off quickly before dressing for breakfast.

An hour later we're packed and out the door with our bags. I barely register the conversation between Creed and the front desk clerk as he checked us out of the hotel. Once again my mind goes to the meeting with the Council of Elders.

• • • •

THE DRIVE TO SHERIDAN Springs town hall does little to quell the anxiety I feel when memories of my first meeting with the Council of Elders was an unpleasant experience. Arriving fifteen minutes before the scheduled 10:00 a.m. meeting gives me time to calm my bear before facing the firing squad known as the Council of Elders. Shamefully, I tell Creed a white lie to claim a moment alone.

"I need the ladies room; will you wait here for me?"

"I'll go with you."

"It's call the ladies room. Men aren't allowed," I teased halfheartedly.

"Which is why I'll wait outside the door for you."

Just as I'm about to protest my father arrives, distracting my mate.

"I'll be right back," I say to my father by way of greeting.

Giving Creed a quick peck on his lips, I excuse myself.

"Where is she off to?" I hear my father ask.

"Ladies room," Creed responds.

Hurriedly, I make my way down the short hall before Creed decides to follow me. Turning the corner as I approach the ladies room I soon realize my mistake when I come face-to-face with Langdon Whitmore.

"I'd hope we'd run into each other before the hearing," he says, blocking my path to the ladies room.

"I'd hope I would never see you again."

An evil grin stretches across his thin lips, prompting me to take a step back. My gaze turns to the direction I came, and I immediately regret my decision to venture the halls of this place alone. There are actual monsters around every corner.

"I can smell your heat, omega," he says, ignoring my comment. "You'll be begging to be fucked soon, and this time nothing will stop me from taking my fill of you. And once this hearing is over I intend to do just that."

I nearly gag, hearing his lewd promise, but manage to maintain my composure. Remembering how our last encounter ended, I make a promise of my own.

"Touch me again and I'll take your head off next time."

When his bear's black eyes return to his natural shade of brown, I dare him by taking a step forward. Challenging an alpha was never my intention, because truthfully the omega in me craves her true alpha. Fortunately for me, my body knows the difference. Now that I've found my fated mate, no other male compares. Without knowing what to expect from Langdon, I turn my back to him and walk away.

I find my mate and my father waiting for me. Creed greets me with a heartwarming smile before extending his hand to me. Accepting his hand, I ask. "Are you ready to vanquish a few ghost?"

"And a monster or two," Creed replies.

Pushing open the creaky wooden double doors, I enter the meeting room of the town hall and once again the eyes of the council members and current alpha, Langdon Whitmore, focus on me. Although I'm not that same naive girl who entered the room nearly four years ago, I know I can count on my mate and my father for support.

"Welcome back, omega," Langdon greets coldly.

"You will address my mate, by her name, or you will not address her at all." Creed growls.

"And you will speak to our alpha with respect or be banned from this meeting." Preema, one of three females on the seven-member council retorts.

Squeezing Creed's hand, I manage to calm the fury of his bear.

"If your alpha, or the council doesn't show Rylie the respect she deserves, threatening to ban me from this meeting for defending my mate will be the least of your concerns."

The unspoken promise in Creed's words leaves no room for misunderstanding. Langdon and the council heeds my mate's warning. Unfortunately, upon hearing Creed claim me as his mate before the council, Langdon's treacherous black eyes meet mine. Ignoring the glare of his bear, I look away when Preema's voice breaks the silence.

"Step forward, Rylie Adams,"

Releasing Creed's hand, I take a few steps forward to face the council's judgement.

"Rylie Adams, you stand accused of forsaking your duties as omega to the Sheridan Springs clan and it's new alpha, Langdon Whitmore. You have been summoned here to account for your actions and face the judgment of the clan's Council of Elders. You may now defend your actions."

Knowing that this will be the first time my mate and my father hear the sorted details of Langdon's attempted rape, I mentally prepare myself for their reactions.

"I didn't choose to be born an omega. However, the Sheridan Springs clan has always made me feel ashamed to be one. Yet, I went along with the council's outdated breeding laws for the betterment of my clan. Fortunately for me I realized my obedience to the council wasn't a reward but a punishment, so I ran away from the lodge before the intrusive examination to determine the levels of my heat and fertility was performed."

"You admit that you ran away of your own free will?" Preema asks.

As one of the two council members guarding me four years ago, I assume she felt responsible for failing to fulfill her duties.

"Yes, I ran away of my own free will. I had no idea where I was going, I just knew I had to get far away as fast as I could. Unfortunately, running away didn't stop an alpha challenger from tracking me to the lodge and deeper into the forest."

"You do realize you've just accused a challenger for alpha of breaking the no contact law?"

"Yes, I'm fully aware."

"Do you intend to name this challenger?"

"Yes, that is my intention."

My eyes go to Langdon of their own volition, and the council members follow suit.

"I'd been running in unfamiliar territory when I caught his scent advancing towards me. That's also when I truly realized I would never be safe within my own clan."

"How can you blame your clan for your lack of safety when you just admitted to running away from the safety of the lodge and the protection of the council?"

Shaking my head free of the memories of Langdon attempt at rape, I repeat his vile threat verbatim to the council.

"It's only a matter of time before I defeat your father. However, I have no problem with stacking the odds in my favor. I intend to be the one to claim your heat, omega. So, even if your father manages to prevail during the alpha challenge you'll still be mine."

"Not even time will let me forget his words or his actions. He believed the rules didn't apply to him and he could defy the council's breeding laws and take whatever he wanted from what you all see as the lowest member of your clan, an omega."

"How did you manage to get away?" Preema asks.

Knowing this part will bruise Langdon's ego, I reveal how he was bested by a lowly omega. "After he pinned me to the ground, I smashed a large stone against his head as hard as I could, twice, before he fell unconscious, and I ran."

"Are you saying you defeated an alpha challenger?"

"I'm saying Langdon Whitmore, broke the rules of the challenge which should have disqualified him. Therefore, he was no longer a challenger for alpha, by his actions not mine."

"She's lying," Langdon accuses. "I was nowhere near the lodge; I was with my father until he was summoned by the council."

"That's right," Beau attest, validating his son's alibi. "The council convened to discuss whether or not to continue the alpha challenge without the omega, since she was missing."

"My mate is not a liar," Creed defends, stepping to my side.

"You say she's your mate, yet you haven't claimed her," Beau responds.

"Unlike the Sheridan Springs clan, my clan values their omegas. They aren't treated as possession. They're honored and cherished. And when it comes to choosing a mate she's free to have more than one if she desires it unless she finds her fated mate."

Creed speaks proudly of his clan, reciting words similar to the ones he said to me. The three female council members let out an audible gasp, While the men huff in frustration.

Standing, Langdon directs his comment to Creed. "Your clan's practices has no bearing on this hearing, therefore your opinion on ours doesn't matter."

The male council members bang their fists down on the table in agreement with their alpha.

Preema's stern voice brings the meeting back to order, but Langdon remains standing.

"In this clan only an alpha can claim an omega, and since Rylie Adams is still a member of our clan she cannot be claim by an outsider," Langdon adds.

"I believe you'll find I'm the exception to the rule," Creed remarks dryly.

"If we can get back to why we're here, we can address the issue of Rylie's assumed mate later," Preema interjects.

"I may be able to shed some light on Rylie's accusations against our alpha," Denna Miles the only omega ever allowed to join the council says, standing to address her fellow council members.

Three of the remaining six council members nod their agreement to Preema, consenting to allow Denna's testimony.

"It was our job, mine and Preema's to keep Rylie safe and hidden until the claiming ceremony. So when I woke and found Rylie wasn't in her bed, I went looking for her. What I didn't expect to find was the scent of an alpha challenger. I forced myself not to imagine the worst, and I kept looking for Rylie, until her omega pheromones gave way to the scent of an alpha challenger's blood, Langdon Whitmore's blood."

"You expect the council to believe the words of a damaged omega?"

Beau's insult visibly affects Denna, but she shakes off his cruel words with grace and dignity.

"Yes, it's true as an omega, I'm considered damaged due to a childhood accident that prevents me from baring cubs. So, I've chosen to serve my clan in a different capacity. And that means putting the clan first above all else. As a council member I take my vow to protect our omegas seriously."

"Do you have any proof the support your allegation?" Preema asks.

"I have the rock with Langdon's blood on it, and photos of the scene where I found it."

"Why haven't you come forward with this supposed proof until now?" Beau snaps.

"I held onto it for her," Denna says, pointing to me. "I didn't know if Langdon killed her or if she just ran away. Either way I knew everything I collected was proof of Langdon's involvement in Rylie's disappearance."

"I invoke my right to challenge Langdon Whitmore for alpha." Creed's voice is a boom silencing the chatter in the room.

"Need I remind the council that this outsider has no right to challenge our alpha," Beau spat venomously.

"Beauregard Whitmore, it is my birthright, by blood and honor to challenge your son, as you challenged my father, the former alpha of the Timber Valley bear clan. It is my right as the son of Sheridan Springs' former omega, Willa Creed, to avenge the murder of my mother's fated mate. It is also my right to challenge anyone who attempts to harm my fated mate."

Shocked by Creed's confession, Denna takes a seat, obviously forgetting her testimony and the proof she claims to have.

"Is any of this true, Beau?" Preema questions. "Did you murder Timber Valley's alpha."

"Go on, Whitmore, tell your fellow council members, how you lost the challenge to my father, in an attempt to claim his fated mate, my mother. Tell them how after you'd lost, you shifted and attacked him from behind and mauled him to death. Tell them how you then proceeded to beat his defenseless five-year-old son within an inch of his life. How you raped and kidnapped my mother, while her child laid dying beside her murdered mate."

Without warning Creed shifts quicker than I've ever seen any shifter do. For a moment my feet stay planted, watching in awe as Creed's Kodiak charge towards Beau. The council of elders, as well as Langdon scurries away, leaving Beau to fend for himself as he falls onto his back. But Creed isn't attacking, instead he pins a defenseless Beau down with one massive paw.

Heedless of the voices shouting for me to stay away, I approach my mate cautiously. Standing directly in his line of sight, I say the first thing that comes to mine.

"Don't let him take your birthright, or your honor from you."

The deep brown eyes of Creed's bear stare down at me, melting my heart with the pain I see within. Stepping closer, I extend my hand, waiting for my mate to take it. I stand vigil, watching as Beau manage to wriggle free when Creed's Kodiak gives way to the man I love.

Breathing a sigh of relief, I go willingly when Creed's large hand wrap around mine and tug me against his naked body. I don't know how long we stood in the empty town hall embracing each other. In hindsight it may have been a little too long if the hard bulge of Creed's cock pressing against my stomach is an indication.

"We need to settle our issues with the council, so we can get back to finding Lorelei." I whisper against Creed's bare chest.

"I need to cover my bare ass before we invite everyone back in."

Laughing, I free myself from Creed's hold before revealing my last secret. I find his tattered jeans on the floor and hold them up for my mate to see. Chanting a spell to restore torn clothing, I watch Creed's expression go from confusion to admiration.

"You can wield the magic of a witch," Creed surmises.

"My magic is taught, but yes, I seem to have a gift for it."

Reaching for his jeans, Creed examines them thoroughly before stepping into them.

"Show me your gift, Goldie."

Without hesitation, I repeat the spell, restoring Creed's shirt and boots.

"How does your clan not see how amazing you are?" Creed asks, pulling me into his arms once again.

"They don't know about my ability to wield magic."

Lowering his head, he whispers. "Your gift with magic isn't what makes you special, Rylie Adams."

"Thank you."

After a few minutes my father is the first to reenter, followed by Preema, Denna, Langdon, Beau and the rest of the council bringing up the rear. My father who has been silent throughout the entire hearing, approach us wearily, but stand with us in a show of support.

"Your fates are now tied together," Preema announces, resuming the hearing as if there wasn't a big ass Kodiak pinning a council member to the floor nearly an hour ago. "The council will grant you seventy-two hours to prepare for the alpha challenge."

I can only assume Creed is satisfied with the council's decision when he takes me by the hand and leads me out the door. Exiting the town hall with Creed and my father at my side, I feel safer than I ever have, surrounded by them.

Outside the town hall, Creed and I say goodbye to my father before heading to Timber Valley.

"We'll be back in a few days for the challenge," Creed assures my father. "In the meantime please send us the time and location the alpha challenge will take place."

With a kiss to my forehead, and a handshake for Creed, my father waves us off.

Chapter 10
Creed

BEHIND THE WHEEL OF my Silverado, I should feel some level of excitement returning to my father's home with my fated mate at my side. Unfortunately, my reason for returning, along with bad memories that out way the good has me on edge. However, when a view of the mountains in the distance tells me I'm getting close, I can't help but to feel a sense of pride for my clan.

Rylie and I filled the distance from Sheridan Springs to Timber Valley with small talk. For more than two hundred miles we avoided the elephant sitting between us. Revealing my connection to Beau Whitmore and Sheridan Springs didn't go as I intended. I wanted to tell Rylie privately. But anger got the better of me, and for a moment I couldn't control my bear. The sight of the man who killed my father, raped and kidnapped my mother awaken a deep seeded hatred I thought I had gotten pass. When I heard Rylie recount how Langdon Whitmore had attempted to sexually assault her, following in his father's heinous footsteps, all I saw were monsters that needed to be put down. However, before I deal with the Whitmore monsters, I need to find the one that took my daughter.

Approaching Timber Valley's town square, I note how not much has changed since I was here four years ago. Timber Valley is one of two small towns in Utah that are bear shifter communities. With a population shy of eight hundred, it's the smallest of the two shifter clans.

"My cousin's garage is just a few blocks over. We'll stop there for any information he may have obtained regarding Stryker's whereabouts."

"Sounds good," Rylie says, taking in a fleeting view of my hometown as she stares out the passenger window. Then she says something that totally catches me off guard. "I think the twins will like it here."

"We can discuss where we'll live once our entire family is together."

Turning away from the window to face me, she says. "They're going to love you as much as I do."

I'm not sure if Rylie meant to profess her love for me or if she's just speaking in terms of general affection. I don't have long to dwell on it or question her feelings for me before the garage come into view. Vowing to explore this topic later, I put my truck in park and climb out.

With Rylie at my side, we enter Masterson Motors, and the familiar sound of engines purring, the off-key tones of my cousin's singing has me feeling nostalgic. Taking a quick look around the garage, I find his radio and turn the volume down.

"You better have a good reason to touch my radio," he shouts from beneath a blue 1966 Mustang convertible in need of some serious restoration.

"Yeah, I do. You're singing is as bad as ever."

Seconds later a big hulk of a man I once towered over now stands toe-to-toe with me. Looking no worse for wear, my cousin pulls me into his bulky tattooed covered arms. With a quick bro clap to my back he releases me.

"It's good to see you, Creed."

"It's good to see you to, Kurt. But I'm not hear for a social visit." His attention goes to Rylie, and she steps closer to me. "We're here to find our daughter."

"Your daughter?" Kurt asks, and I hear the shock in his questioning tone.

"Yes, she was kidnapped by a bear shifter known as Stryker two days ago."

Ignoring me, Kurt turns his attention to Rylie once again. This time my bear inches forward, asserting his dominance.

"Retract those claws, cousin, I'm just teasing."

When my bear refuses to back down, Rylie takes my hand in hers, attempting to soothe the possessive beast in me.

"I'm Rylie Adams, Creed's fated mate and mother to his cubs."

"Did you say cubs?"

"Yes, twins, a boy and a girl. Our daughter was kidnapped, so we've come to you for any information you have on Stryker. We tracked his last known location to Timber Valley."

"A fated mate and twin cubs, you've been busy, cousin."

"Which means I didn't come here to waste my time," I growl.

Knowing from experience once the clock starts ticking on an abduction the chances of finding my daughter reduces significantly after the first forty-eight hours. We're now approaching hour fifty-five.

Nodding, Kurt seems to realize this is no time for childish taunts.

"Pops has what you're looking for. He's up at the main house."

"Thank you," Rylie says, tugging me out the door.

Outside the garage, away from Kurt's prying eyes, I pin Rylie against my truck. In a surge of magnetic passion my lips are drawn to hers. Fueled by untamable desire, my need for her grows exponentially.

"You're mine, Rylie Adams," I groan hungrily against her lips.

"I'm yours, Creed Masterson," she pants breathlessly.

My mate's words satisfies my bear for now, allowing me to cage him once again.

"The main house isn't far," I let Rylie know once I'm finally able to release her.

The drive to my family's homestead puts us closer to the edge of the forest that leads to my cabin. Another place I haven't visited since the time I spent there with Rylie four years ago. Driving up to the main house, my sight goes to the two Gambel oak trees in the front yard. My feet barely have time to touch the ground before two women with identical faces come bounding down the steps.

"Creed!" They yell excitedly in harmony."

Unable to hold back my smile, I scoop them both up in my arms. My sister's giggles remind me of what home was like before our parents were taken away from us. Three years younger than me, my sisters are omegas, just like our mother and my fated mate. Although Tessa has found her fated mate and has four cubs of her own, Jessica prefers to have multiple mates.

"Kurt called to say you were coming. It's so good to see you, brother," Tessa says.

"He also said you have a surprise for us," Jessica adds.

Placing them firmly on their feet, I turn to my truck, beckoning Rylie to join us. The passenger door opens, and my sisters beam up at me and back to Rylie.

"Rylie these are my sisters, Tessa and Jessica."

"Nice to meet you both," Rylie greets, shaking their hands one after the other.

"Tess, Jess, this is Rylie Adams, my fated mate."

"I always wanted a sister," Jess teases, nudging her twin sister playfully.

"Me too," Rylie laughs.

"Come on inside!" I hear a familiar voice yell from the doorway.

"That's uncle Frank." The twin say to Rylie in unison.

Rylie laughs and the twins smile, taking my mate by her hands. They escort her up the steps to the front door and into the house. Following close behind them, I'm there before the twins introduce Rylie to our uncle.

Franklin Masterson took on the role of clan alpha when my father died. A role he never wanted, but one I wasn't ready for at five years old. A role I'm still not sure I'm ready for. After making the introductions, my sisters excuse themselves and Rylie, Frank and I get down to why we're here.

"What do you have for us?" I ask, once I'm sure my sisters are not within earshot.

"Not very much, I'm sorry to say. We know Stryker arrived two days ago..."

"Do you know if he's traveling with a little blonde girl," Rylie interrupts.

"We don't know if he's traveling with anyone. Our trackers haven't been able to locate him since he got to town, but we know where he'll be late tonight."

"Where?" Rylie asks hopefully.

"I have it on good authority that he'll be attending a private poker game at Chesties."

"Can you get me in?" I ask.

"Can you get us in?" Rylie interjects.

"Sorry, Rylie, no females allowed," Frank says.

"I can't just do nothing; it will drive me crazy."

"We're in this together, but I have to do this part alone. I also need to know you're safe."

Nodding, Rylie acquiesces, and Franklin takes the opportunity to change the subject.

"In the meantime head upstairs and get settled, dinner will be ready in a few hours."

"We're not staying, but we'll join you for dinner."

"Good enough," Frank says. "While we wait for dinner you may as well show Rylie around the property."

Taking my uncle's advice, I take Rylie on a tour of the property. Without fully realizing it, I end the tour in the place where my nightmares began. Approaching the rustic treehouse cottage I feel my father's presence in the air, whispering words of encouragement.

"This place was once my sanctuary." I hear myself confessing to Rylie. "Until my father's death, he and I would camp out here during the summer."

As if sensing I have more to say, Rylie leads me up the ladder to the top of the treehouse. Peeking through the branches of the trees, we gaze at the view of the mountains in silence for long seconds before I find my words again.

"I was here in my treehouse when I heard my mother's screams. My father warned me to stay inside that day, but I disobeyed him. By the time I climbed down and ran into the forest, Whitmore was shifting, and all I could do was watch as his grizzly charged my father from behind and pinned him down as he pounded him into the earth. My mother dropped to her knees and begged him to stop. When my mother promised to leave us, I began to cry. My five-year-old mind couldn't understand why my mother was willing to leave us and go away with a monster. Whitmore ignored both our tears that day. When I woke from a coma a week later, my father had already been buried and my mother was gone. Whitmore kept her away from us for nearly a year, and when she came back she was never the same. She grieved my father for twenty-five years before she finally succumb to grief and took her own life."

The phantom pain of my memories drop me to my knees as I release an agonizing growl. Caught between grief and rage, I jump from the treehouse to avoid hurting my mate. My feet hit the ground and I let the shift happen, freeing myself from a torrent of emotions.

• • • •

FOR SEVERAL HOURS I give control over to my bear and allow him to roam the familiar territory of the Timber Valley clan. Deep in the forest my mate's scent calls to me. Tracking the intoxicating allure of Rylie's omega pheromones my need to rut grows stronger the closer I get to her.

Spying my cabin in the distance the moonlight is a beacon to my fated mate. A rush of excitement fuels my desire and I race towards my destiny. Reaching the cabin door, my bear sniffs the air before surrendering his freedom.

With a firm push, the door swings open, and I step inside. When I enter the cabin Rylie is there waiting for me. Vivid blue eyes dance over my naked body with a surge of heat that races straight to my cock. Aware that my mate is in full blown heat, I manage to ignore my own aching needs, and wait for Rylie to take the lead.

Relief floods my veins, when she strips away her jeans and T-shirt, baring herself to me.

"I want to share my heat with you, Creed."

Rylie's voice is strong and confident, a far cry from the naïve young shifter who asked me to share her first heat four years ago.

"You understand what you're asking of me? What this means for us?"

"I'm asking you to claim me as your fated mate, to share my heat, and the next and the next for the rest of our lives."

My mate's seductive strides close the space between us, and I give myself permission to claim what's mine. When eagerness and desperation lengthens my cock seeking Rylie's heat, I scoop her up into my arms. Instinctively her legs circle my waist, her arms wrap around my neck and her warm wet core grinds against the muscles of my abs. The feel of her body surrounding mine is almost too much to handle, causing my bear to rattle the cabin walls with a fierce growl. Unimaginable pleasure hardens my cock and tightens my balls, and before I can stop myself my seed spills to the floor.

When Rylie's hips stop moving I mentally chastise myself for performing like an inexperienced school boy.

"Don't you dare stop, " I command. "Take what you need from me."

"I don't want you to waste it. I want your seed inside me."

Rylie's breathless confession causes my heart to race with excitement, as I imagine her belly swelling with my cub. Knowing that I want nothing more than to douse her heat with my seed and fill her belly with as many cubs as she can bear. I vow never to waste my seed again.

"It won't happen again," I promise.

I carry Rylie to our bed locked in a desperately passionate embrace. As she clings to me our flesh melds together making it difficult to determine where she begins, and I end. Sandwiched between the mattress and my body, Rylie spread her legs wide for me. Effortlessly, my cock finds the source of my mate's heat. Sinking deep into the depths of Rylie's fiery core my body shudders on contact. For a moment, I stay planted, unmoving, enjoying the feel of my mate after being without her for so many years. When her hips begin to move wildly, I know she's seeking relief from the heat consuming her. Thrust after thrust I pound into her, targeting the spot that will be our undoing. Waves of pleasure quake my soul with the force of my seed ejecting from my body. Rylie's body responds with a rush of heat enveloping my cock.

"More, Creed! More!"

Rylie's fevered demands, along with the feel of her spasming core, sends me into uncontrollable rut. Our bodies collide finding the rhythm to our souls, and I drive deeper. My strokes become harder and faster fueled by my mate's rising heat. The sounds of our grunts and moans fill the air in the cabin. It's pure ecstasy; unlike anything I've ever experience before.

"Fuck," I growl unable to find the words to describe the bliss my mate gives me.

"Yes, Creed, fuck me. Fuck me harder, I need every inch of your big cock buried deep inside me."

Raising her hips to meet my thrusts, Rylie cries out when I slam into her unleashing a blazing inferno. The searing passion between us becomes an inevitable explosion needing release. My mind and body gives way to our mate bond, and once again my heart beats in sync with my fated mate's. Instinctively my knot swells inside Rylie, and the urge to consummate the mate bond triggers just like it had four years ago. This time there's no fighting it, I allow my knot to take hold of Rylie, as I claim my fated mate fully. My seed spills from me as Rylie's core spasms around my cock. Pulse after pulse I fill her until my body deflates against hers.

Slowly my knot disappears, freeing Rylie from its hold, allowing my cock to slip free of her body. Greedily, the moment my cock leaves the warmth of my mate's heat, I want back in. Instead I roll onto my back, pulling Rylie into my arms. For a few heart pounding moments we lie panting as are breathing returns to normal.

"Forgive me for leaving you alone in the treehouse. I was afraid my bear would hurt you."

"There's nothing to forgive. And your bear would never hurt me, Creed."

"No, I suppose not."

"Thank you for sharing your past with me. Knowing you better makes me love you all the more."

Hearing Rylie say for the second time she loves me, has me confessing my true feelings for her. "I never thought I'd find my fated mate, and when I did, losing you devastated me."

"You never lost me, Creed. I just needed to find myself."

"I love you, Rylie Adams."

"I love you too."

"Will you do me the honor of completing my clan's traditional bonding ceremony?"

"Are you asking me to marry you, Creed Masterson."

Rylie's stomach grumbles, postponing my response for now.

"We missed dinner," she offers as an explanation for her hunger.

"I doubt there's anything in the cupboard, I haven't been back here since..."

"I left." Rylie assumes correctly. "Why?"

Vowing to have no more secrets between my mate and myself, I tell a necessary truth.

"When I arrived and found you in my cabin it was also the day of my mother's burial service. She had taken her own life the week before. I came here to be alone, to mourn the loss of my mother privately."

"I'm sorry, I didn't know."

"How could you have known. Regardless, finding you here became a welcome distraction and I'll never regret our time together. I knew you were my fated mate, so when you left without saying goodbye, it felt like I was mourning the loss of both of you all at once. The pain of it was too overwhelming."

"I never meant to hurt you."

"I know. But I didn't realize until after I spent time repairing the cabin that we had to travel our different paths alone."

"What happened to the cabin."

"Let's just say my bear and I didn't take your rejection well."

Eager to lay the topic to rest, I attempt to untangle my body from Rylie's. "Why do you smell so good?" My mate asks, stopping me with the brush of her lips against my neck.

"Alpha pheromones. You can smell it now that we've consummated our mate bond, and you will smell it as long as you're in heat."

"So you're truly an alpha?"

"It's my birthright."

"That means we have a true alpha-omega mate bond," Rylie manage to say between bouts of laughter.

"Why is that so funny?"

"There hasn't been a true alpha-omega mate bond within the Sheridan Springs clan for three generations. Yet somehow, me, the last omega of my clan has managed to find her fated mate and give birth to the next generation's true alpha and omega."

"Like I said, how can your clan not see how absolutely amazing you are."

Rylie's full pouty lips morphs into a genuine smile for the first time since our daughter was taken. The kind that reaches her eyes and melts my heart.

"I guess they're too busy to see beyond their own agenda to ensure the clan's magic at all cost to see me as more than just an omega."

"Then that's their mistake."

"Yes it is, but they will benefit from our union, nonetheless." I hear the resentment in Rylie's voice when she adds. "Including the Whitmores."

"The Whitmores will soon get what they deserve, I can promise you that."

Refusing to allow past traumas to take any more time from our intimate moment, I ask my mate to tell me more about our cubs."

"What are they like?" Logan and Lorelei, what are they like?"

With a heartwarming smile she says. "I'll tell you all about them over dinner."

"Dinner?" I question.

"Yes, your sisters brought dinner to the treehouse for us when we didn't return to the main house."

"Is that how you ended up here, my sisters brought you to the cabin?"

"Tessa told me you like to come here to be alone."

"I used to, now I like being here with you."

"When I walked in, it was like coming home, and I knew in my heart I was meant to find my mate here." It just took me some time to find my way back to you." Rylie confesses.

Climbing out of bed, I accept Rylie's extended hand, following her to the living area. That's when I notice the large picnic basket atop the small table near the wood burning stove. My stomach growls anticipating the meal, as my eyes feast on the appetizing view of my mate's gloriously naked body.

Over dinner I listen intently as Rylie regales me on the virtues of our children, loving how vividly she paints the picture of their personalities, it makes me feel in some small way I was there to witness their milestones.

"Thank you for sharing your memories of Logan and Lorelei with me."

"You'll make your own memories with them soon, until then I'm more than happy to share mine with you."

"Until then let's get you back to the main house were its safe."

"I can wait here until you get back."

"I need to know you're safe, or I can't do what I need to do to get our daughter back."

"There's no one else around for miles."

"Exactly."

I would lose my fucking mind if something were to happen to my fated mate. If the mark of my alpha pheromones failed to deter an unmated male shifter away from Rylie, an omega in heat.

"Besides, there's safety in numbers, my sisters can look after you while I'm away. And the three of you can get to know each other better." I add, hoping she doesn't insist on staying in the cabin alone.

"Alright, I'll stay at the main house with Tess and Jess."

Standing I give Rylie an eye bulging view of my erect cock. "But, not until I've doused your heat a bit more."

"Oh yes, please," Rylie practically moans.

I don't know how long Rylie and I stay entangled in a fevered haze of passion before coming up for air. What I do know is tonight has proven I'll never let her go.

Chapter 11
Rylie

WHEN CREED AND I ENTER the main house, members of his clan, Franklin, Kurt, Tess and Jess, along with several other male shifters greet us. Without cause Creed growls, putting himself between me and the shifters. Kurt and a few other males take a step back as if the force of an alpha's dominance demanded them to do so.

Breaking the tension in the room Tessa steps forward with a handsome dark hair male shifter at her side.

"Brother, this is my mate, Wade Connor?" She says, holding Wade's left hand.

With a slight bow of his head Wade extends his free hand to Creed. A moment of silence pass between them and I begin to wonder if Creed would accept Wade's gesture of greeting.

"It's so good to meet you," Wade says.

Finally, Creed responds. "It's good to meet you as well, Wade."

Shaking hands the two shifters seem to come to an unspoken understanding. Wade isn't a threat Creed has to protect me from. Unlike the other male shifters in the room, Wade is already mated.

"It's time we discuss how we're going to proceed," Franklin says, gaining our attention. "Creed, unfortunately, I wasn't able to wrangle you a last-minute invite to the poker game."

Nodding his acceptance, Creed says, "I don't need entry into the poker game, all I need is Stryker to show up at Chesties."

"Which is why I've called a few clan members here to back you up," Franklin adds.

Looking over the assembled clan members, Creed makes a visual assessment of the shifters before him.

"Kurt and Wade will back me up," Creed decides. "Since there's a chance Stryker isn't working alone, the females and cubs will stay inside the main house until this is over."

"I'll leave the others behind to secure the homestead," Franklin agrees.

Hearing Creed insist his sisters and I, along with Tess and Wade's cubs should stay inside, Jess voices her heated opinion against the restriction.

"We're not helpless omegas, brother," Jess counters. "Since we were just cubs, you've made sure Tess, and I could defend ourselves. And from what I've heard your mate is no pushover, she's already fought this Stryker and lived to tell the tale."

I witness Creed's verbal sparring with his sister give way to the visceral command of a true alpha. "You will stay here with Rylie and Jess, do you understand?" Creed's tone is firm, and there's no mistaking the authority behind it. "I will not lose anyone else I love, Jess." he adds.

As Jess's eyes lower in submission to her brother, recognizing him as a true alpha, I knew someday soon my mate would lead his clan.

With everyone in agreement, Franklin left for the poker game, Wade escorted Tess upstairs to check in on their sleeping cubs. I'm not sure where Jess disappeared to, but Kurt hustled the unmated male shifters out the door. Left alone with Creed, I share my concerns for his safety.

"I wish there was more I could do to help you."

"Knowing you'll be safe while I'm away helps me more than you can imagine."

"Lorelei is our daughter; I should be the one backing you up."

"And you're my mate," Creed growls. "I'd die before I allow that monster to take you as well. So let me get our daughter back for us both."

"I'd die if I loss you and Lorelei to Stryker."

In attempt to banish our mutual fear of losing Lorelei and each other, Creed's lips crash against mine. The smoldering fire between us begins to blaze to an inferno. I go weak in the knees from the pressure of his mouth, and the demands of his sweeping tongue.

When Creed lifts me off my feet effortlessly, moans of pure delight escapes my throat. Rejoicing, I wrap my legs around his waist eager for the feel of his muscular abs against my throbbing center. Pure instinct has me grinding against my mate wantonly, needing desperately to extinguish the heat rising within me.

Without warning the sure stride of heavy footsteps carry me away. For a moment with my eyes closed, and my body taking and receiving pleasure from Creed's, the snick of a door locking doesn't quite register. At least not until Creed's mouth leaves mine. Planting me firmly on my feet, Creed tugs my jeans down before freeing is massively engorged cock.

"This will have to do until I return," he whisper growls. "Bend over and hold on to the sink."

I wish I could say his command was a turnoff, but the way he looks at me only causes my core to quiver ravenously with need. Doing as my mate commands, I turn my back to Creed and grab hold of the sink. Facing the mirrored reflection of my mate, his moonlit gray eyes draws me in. I watch with anticipation as Creed positions himself behind me. Hard and fast he plunges into me, filling an ache deep within my core.

Penetrating thrusts push me over the edge so fast I'm unable to contain the deep moans or the mating growl of my bear as I shatter into a million pieces.

"I fucking love that sound, Goldie."

Creed's bearish grunts echoes off the walls of the half-bath as he follows me over the edge. Sated for now, his tight hold on my hips becomes a gentle caress. From the mirror I watch the eyes of our bears retreat, giving way to the bright blue of mine and the silvery gray of my mate's.

Pulling his cock free of the heat that's starting to build in my core once again, Creed takes a few steps away from me before tucking himself back into his jeans. My eyes lower, hiding my need from my mate as I mourn the loss of his possession. Aware that Creed is watching me, I busy myself with righting my appearance. Tugging my jeans up over my hips, I continue to avoid my mate's inquisitive gaze. Realizing I'll have to look at him at some point, it may as well be now.

Turning away from the mirror to face Creed, I ask. "Why can't I get enough?"

"Once you're heat passes we won't be driven to mate as much," Creed explains.

"So, I only feel like this because I'm in heat."

"We're fated mates, we will always feel this intensely for each other, but that overwhelming need to mate will subside when your heat does."

"And this will happen every time I go into heat?"

"It will."

A knock on the bathroom door startles me and I forget my next question.

"Yes." Creed calls to the person on the other side of the door.

"Wade and Kurt are ready when you are."

"Thank you, Tess," Creed replies.

The sound of Tessa's retreating footsteps has me wrapping my arms around Creed and shoving aside my unanswered questions for now.

"Walk with me to the truck," he whispers comfortingly.

I nod my agreement, and we leave the bathroom hand-in-hand.

Stepping out into the night air, the starlit sky winks with endless possibilities, while the moon promises the impossible.

Tessa steals my attention away from the moon and the stars when I hear her promise to Wade. "Come back to me and I'll give you a son," she vows.

"I'm going to hold you to that, Tessa Masterson," Wade says, before planting a kiss on her lips.

Turning away from the mated pair, I notice Creed smiling at the couple.

"They have four daughters," Creed shares.

"I'll make whatever promises to whatever deity that will hear my prayer, all I ask is that they send you back to me and we get Lorelei back."

"Promise me you'll stay inside where it's safe."

"I'll stay inside. I promise."

Pushing up on my tiptoes, my mouth hovers beneath Creed's until he lowers his head. I intended our kiss to be brief, but the toe-curling caress of his lips will always be my undoing. Kurt clears his throat, and I find the strength to back away from my fated mate.

Suddenly it occurs to me that there's a way for me to help Creed and the others. While my magic is something I had to learn to wield, it has never failed me. Although I'm not able to command the elements like Aria, or create new spells like Naomi, the spells and incantations I've learned from these powerful witches are the core of my magical gift.

"I need your handcuffs." Ignoring Creed's confused expression, I clarify. "May I hold your handcuffs, please?"

Reaching into the glove box, Creed retrieves his handcuffs.

Relief fills me when he hands over two sets of cuffs. With the handcuffs in the palm of my left hand, I cover them with my right. Closing my eyes, I chant a spell of illusion. My spell will cause the wearer to see the handcuffs as inescapable shackles. When I open my eyes, I have the unwanted attention of Creed's family.

"I gave these a little something special. Stryker won't be able to escape them, and he'll yield to your command."

"Let's go!" Kurt shouts.

"Go on inside," Creed says, after placing a tender kiss on my forehead.

Once I'm on the porch, I wait for Creed and the others to drive off. When they stay put, I turn to Tess.

"Wade and Kurt won't leave without Creed, and Creed won't leave until you're inside the house."

Understanding dawns, as my mate's words play on a loop in my head.

"I need to know you're safe, or I can't do what I need to do to get our daughter back. Knowing you'll be safe while I'm away helps me more than you can imagine."

It's times like this I wish Creed and I had the ability to speak telepathically like Aria and her mates, the Westwood triplets. Resigning myself to the fact the Creed has to leave me behind for the sake of our daughter, I follow Tess into the house.

• • • •

WITH CREED OUT TRACKING down Stryker, the shifter who took our daughter, his sisters, twins, Tess and Jess, attempts at distracting me is appreciated, but it doesn't stop my mind from returning to my mate and our daughter. Lorelei has been missing two and a half days, nothing they do diverts my attention away from that horrible truth.

"So, you're a magic wielder?" Tess blurts out.

"She's a what?" Jess asks, reentering the room with a large tray of snacks.

"A wielder of magic," Tess replies.

"I've learned a few spells," I confess.

"What spell did you use on the handcuffs?" Tess asks curiously.

"An illusion spell."

Placing the tray of snacks atop the large round coffee table, Jess takes a seat on the couch beside me. "How does the spell work?" She asks.

"The spell will cause the wearer to see something that isn't actually there. In this case a pair of ordinary handcuffs becomes a pair of inescapable shackles."

"Not even a pair of shackles will make a shifter compliant," Jess warns.

"I know, which is why I added a second layer to the spell. Once Creed handcuffs Stryker he will be compelled to obey his captor's commands."

"In this case, Creed," Tess surmises.

"Yes, exactly."

"That's some wicked power you have, Rylie," Tess comments.

"And by wicked she means freaking awesome!" Jess exclaims.

"Hell yeah I mean awesome," Tess agrees.

"Now that we're sisters maybe you could teach me a spell or two," Jess winks conspiratorially.

I don't have the heart to tell Jess, her ability to wield magic will likely never manifest. Unlike the Sheridan Springs clan most shifters don't rely on the magic of an alpha-omega union. Unfortunately, I don't know why it's true of my clan, but it has always been that way. Either by curse or creation, the Sheridan Springs clan is dependent upon the alpha-omega union to remain shifters.

"How old are your cubs?" I ask Tess, diverting our conversation away from magic.

Smiling broadly, she answers. "They're two years old."

"And their all omegas?" I ask unable to hide the worry in my tone.

"According to our clan's physician they are."

"My daughter, Lorelei is also an omega." I add tearfully. "She's nearly four years old."

Imagining my sweet Lorelei being subjected to the breeding laws that forced me to run away from my clan, my tears begin to flow freely. Tears I thought I'd shed long ago resurface in a flood of emotions, as uncontrollable sobs rack my body. It's not until I feel Tess and Jess hugging me and comforting me on opposite sides, that I begin to allow myself to actually let go of my old ideas of what an omega should be and embrace what we truly are.

"We've all heard the stories of how the Sheridan Springs clan mistreats their omegas." Jess says empathetically. "We are not just omegas meant for breeding, Rylie. We are also strong, compassionate independent shifters with a capacity for great love."

Listening to Jess put my thoughts into words forces my tears to give way to the expanding of my heart as it makes room for my newfound sisters. With my sobs reduced to intermittent sniffles, we allow a moment of bonding silence to solidify our sisterhood before Tess and Jess release me but remain at my side holding my hand.

"Thank you," I say to them both, giving their hand a gentle squeeze.

"That's what sisters are for," Tess smiles warmly.

Deciding now is as good a time as any to get some answers to my questions, I go for it.

"Can I ask you both a personal question?"

The twins give each other a united nod, before saying. "Ask us whatever you want."

"How do you handle the constant need to mate when you're in heat?"

"I fuck until I've had enough," Jess shares. "That's one of the perks of having multiple mates during my heat."

"I was a late bloomer, I didn't get my first heat until after I'd already found Wade, my fated mate," Tess confesses.

"And how do you keep from getting pregnant every time you go into heat?"

"Rylie," Jess calls my name gaining my full attention. "Hasn't anyone ever told you any of this before now?"

Shamefully, I lower my head in an unsuccessful attempt to hide my ignorance.

"Then it's time we educated you, sister," Tess says. "We get our heat every six months, during that time we have a few options, abstain, which I don't recommend because it can become quite painful."

"Or you can fuck freely with or without the aid of birth control," Jess adds, I choose the latter, because I'm not ready for cubs just yet."

Intrigued, I ask. "Will you tell me about the birth control?"

"Sure, but what did you do before to prevent pregnancies?" Tess asks.

"Spells and potions, I got from a witch friend."

"Is that how you got into magic?" Jess questions.

"Yes it is. Six months after I gave birth to my cubs, I experienced my heat for the second time. The pain was so unbearable, I turned to Naomi, a witch, for help. She didn't hesitate to come to my aid. She taught me how to blend the herbs I needed to block my scent, and an incantation to suppress my heat. So, when she offered to help me tap into the magic of my clan's alpha-omega bond, I agreed."

"Is that the source of your magic, the alpha-omega bond you have with our brother?"

"Creed is my fated mate, but I didn't know of his alpha birthright until recently. I had always assumed it was the inherit magic of my parent's alpha-omega union."

"The fact that Creed is your fated mate and an alpha gives your magic a boost, I'm sure of it," Tess says.

"Which means I'll remain magicless," Jess pouts.

"Unfortunately, sister, that's exactly what it means," Tess teases.

"Honestly, I'm not sure how my magic will affect Creed or our mate bond."

"Now that you're mated do you plan to move to Timber Valley?"

"We haven't really had time to discuss where we'll live. Our focus has been on getting Lorelei back."

"Of course it has, it was foolish of me to ask," Tess says apologetically.

"It's not foolish. It's just that beyond being fated mates, and parents to twin cubs, Creed and I haven't had time to really discuss our future together or what that means for us as a family."

"I'm not sure if Creed has told you how our mother left the Sheridan Springs clan when she found her fated mate, our father, in the Timber Valley clan." Tess continues. He was a young alpha, but he was determined to find his fated mate even if it meant searching for her outside of Timber Valley.

When he found her she was already promised to a member of the Sheridan Springs clan. Normally, that would have made any member of the Timber Valley clan backoff, but she was my father's fated mate and an omega, which meant even the breeding laws of Sheridan Springs couldn't keep them apart. So my mother chose to stay in Timber Valley with my father."

Knowing that omegas aren't permitted to leave Sheridan Springs, I had to ask. "Why had your mother come to Timber Valley?"

"Our grandfather held a celebration to announce our father as the clan's new alpha, and he invited neighboring bear shifter clans."

"Which included Sheridan Springs."

"Yes, the invitation was extended to the entire clan. Initially, they kept their omegas away from the celebration until my grandfather took offense. Omegas of Timber Valley are honored and respected, so he considered it an insult to our clan when Sheridan Springs excluded the omegas of their clan."

"I think your mother was one of the last omegas of the Sheridan Springs clan before I was born."

"That makes since, our mother, Willa, was one of two omegas from the Sheridan Springs clan. According to the stories, the other hadn't experienced her first heat. What was her name..."

"Lorelei Logan," I provide, cutting Tess off, although I knew her question wasn't meant for me. "Her name was Lorelei Logan, my mother."

"Oh, Rylie, I'm so so sorry," Tess stammers.

"No need to apologize," I assure her.

Nodding, she continues. "Needless to say my parents found each other that night only to be torn apart five years later. Our mother was taken from us the day our father died. Jess and I were no older than my cubs are now," Tess chokes out.

"Even when she returned to us, we never got to know her. For twenty-five years her time was spent in isolation grieving our father," Jess finishes for her sister. "Believe me when I say we know the heartache of growing up without a mother and having someone you love taken away from you. With that said, you must know that Creed will do whatever it takes to get Lorelei back and reunite his family. And where you go from there is up to you, but just know that Timber Valley is now your home too."

"Thank you both for welcoming me into your family. I can't wait for Lorelei and Logan to meet their twin aunts."

"And we can't wait to meet them," Tess and Jess say in harmony.

Smiling, I share my observation with them. "Logan and Lorelei often say the same thing at the same time. I call it their twin power."

Laughing, Jess says, "I knew I had magical powers."

Tess and I are pulled into the vortex of Jessa's contagious laughter and for a few peaceful moments I forget my worries.

Chapter 12
Creed

BY MIDNIGHT, I'M PARKED outside Chesties, a shifter biker bar on the outskirts of town, waiting impatiently for Stryker, the bastard who kidnapped my daughter to show up. When Frank was unable to obtain a last-minute invitation for me to join the poker game, he insisted I take back up. While he waits inside for Stryker at the poker table, my cousin Kurt, and Wade Connor, my sister Tessa's fated mate, stake out the back entrance of Chesties.

Moments after a black pickup truck enters the parking lot, a hulking male I recognize as Stryker climbs out. Reaching for the handcuffs, animal instincts shouts for me to shift and rip his throat out for daring to lay a hand on my mate and take our daughter. Instead, I grab a tranquilizer gun and the handcuffs Rylie spelled to be inescapable. I didn't question her when she gave them to me because I didn't have to. She's well aware that human restraints won't hold a bear shifter.

"I gave these a little something special," she said. "Stryker won't be able to escape them, and he'll yield to your command."

The battle to control my primal predatory nature becomes more difficult the closer I get to Stryker. Seeing me advancing he tosses his half-smoked cigarette to the ground. But all I see is red when a sadistic grin curls his lips as if he recognizes me. Instincts tells me he's repairing to shift, and I should as well. Unfortunately, killing this monster isn't the objective. Forcing my bear to remain in his cage, I go with option two. I aim for his torso, firing three times in rapid succession. When that fails to drop the beast to his knees, I unload the rest. With less than minimal satisfaction I watch Stryker's body fall to the ground in a loud thud.

Capturing Stryker was anticlimactic, cuffing him I heft him over my shoulder and toss him into the backseat of my truck. I spare a few seconds to search his pockets, finding only the key to his pickup. I make my way back to Stryker's vehicle, climbing in hoping to find a GPS navigation system that might lead me to Lorelei, but no such luck. The old pickup only has an outdated A.M. radio installed. Leaving the key behind in the driver's seat, I send a quick text to Kurt, letting him know I have Stryker in custody and I'm heading back to the main house. Within seconds my phone rings with a call from my cousin.

"Did Rylie's mojo with the cuffs work?" He asks and I hear the curiosity in his voice.

"I haven't had the chance to test it yet. I'll know once the tranquilizers wear off."

"Well that's one way to take down a bear," Kurt laughs.

"Wade, I left the key to his black pickup truck in the driver's seat. Drive it back to the main house."

"Will do," Wade responds.

"We'll be right behind you," Kurt says before ending the call.

As we approach the entry road to the main house Stryker begins to stir. With him waking I now have an opportunity to test the validity of Rylie's spell. From the rearview mirror, I watch him rouse fully.

Struggling to break free of the cuffs, he shouts. "These won't fucking hold me for long!"

"I don't need them to hold you long. Now sit still and shut up," I command.

Disbelief drains some of the malice from Stryker's eyes, when he realizes he's unable to resist my command.

Kurt and Wade pull up behind me as I'm unloading Stryker from my truck. Climbing out of Stryker's old beat-up truck, Wade is the first to reach me. However, it's my captive he can't seem to look away from. When he finally looks me in the eye, I can tell he has questions for me, and I give him credit for being wise enough not to ask them in front of Stryker."

"I need to go check..."

Understanding Wade's concern for his mate and cubs, all of whom are omegas, I cut him off. "I'll see you inside."

Wade gives me a brief nod, leaving just as Kurt approaches.

"What's with him?" Kurt asks, oblivious to Wade's concerns.

Ignoring Kurt, and eager to get some answers, I shove Stryker towards the barn. However, when Rylie's scent fills the air and the beast who dared to touch her turns in her direction all my questions gets pushed aside.

"Take him to the barn," I growl, issuing the command to Kurt. "Now!"

Hastily, Kurt leads Stryker away, but his eyes remain fixed on my mate as she descends the steps of the front porch.

Stalking towards Rylie, I meet her half way. And before I'm able to think better of it, I'm grabbing her by the upper arm, and dragging her back into the house away from Stryker's prying eyes.

"Slow down, Creed," she says, stumbling as she attempts to keep up with my long-hurried strides.

Determination prevents me from uttering a word until I get Rylie inside. I pick her up as if she weighs nothing. Tossing her over my shoulder, I ignore her pleas to put her down. When the front door swings open, Jess wisely steps aside giving me a wide berth. Effortlessly, I climb the stairs three at a time carrying Rylie to my old bedroom and lock the door behind me.

"Creed."

For long seconds I stand there with my mate resting atop my shoulder, unable to move from beneath the cloud of ominous fury brought on by the dark emotions I'm feeling.

"I'm safe, Creed. You can put me down now."

Somehow hearing Rylie say she's safe, expels my cloud of emotions and cages the furious beast lurking within me.

Placing Rylie steady on her feet, I back away.

"I need to question Stryker, and you need to stay inside like you promised."

"I have a right to be there while you're questioning him."

"Not if it interferes with my ability to think rationally."

"I promise not to interfere with the interrogation, just let me be there."

"Rylie, No!" I shout. "I can't have you near him. It's taking everything in me to keep from ripping his fucking head off. And now he's scented you and seen you."

"He's restrained, Creed. He can't get to me."

"But you can get to him, and every unmated shifter within a fifty-mile radius."

"My heat," she says as understanding dawns.

"Although you're mated, that won't deter a heinous monster like Stryker."

"I need answers just as badly as you do, Creed."

"Then let me get them for the both of us, so we can get our daughter back."

"Lorelei has been gone nearly three days. What if.."

"No what ifs, we will get her back."

Pulling Rylie into my arms, I whisper a promise to her I intend to keep.

Chapter 13
Rylie

WAKING ALONE, I DIDN'T need to wonder where Creed has gone, I already know. He has promised to bring our daughter back home to us. And if Stryker has the answers, I have no doubt Creed has ways of making him talk. Taking in my surroundings, the view of my mate's bedroom is much different from when Creed hauled me in over his shoulder a few hours ago.

Although the room is surprisingly warm and cozy, the massive bed feels lonely without Creed beside me. Climbing out of bed, I make my way down the stairs. When I enter the family room Tess and Jess are where I left them, curled up at opposite ends of the couch fast asleep.

The sound of Creed's thundering voice followed by a pained growl has me forgetting my promise to stay inside. Racing toward the front door, I yank it open only to discover Wade standing as a sentry.

"What was that?" I ask when Wade turns to face me.

"Creed is questioning Stryker, but he's not very talkative." Another pained growl fills the pre-dawn air, and I step forward. Blocking my path, Wade says, "You should go back inside, Rylie."

Deciding not to waste any more time butting heads with stubborn males, I back away from the open door, closing it behind me. What I need is a plan of action that will get my daughter back. That means I need to find a way to get Stryker talking. Retrieving my cell phone from the end table where I left it charging, I hesitated for a moment before calling Naomi for advice.

It's nearly 3 a.m. in Westwood, an hour behind Timber Valley, so I hope she'll forgive my intrusion. Fortunately, she sounds fully alert when she answers without preamble on the first ring.

"Aria said you would be calling."

Aware that Aria, a witch-wolf hybrid and Naomi's niece is able to see glimpses of the future, I want to ask if she's seen Lorelei in her visions. I stop myself from asking when I realize Naomi would have told me if she had.

"What can I do to help?"

"Creed and I have found the shifter who kidnapped Lorelei, but he's not talking."

"Have you tried using a confession spell, or a truth spell?"

"No, I haven't. But I've used and illusion spell on handcuffs to keep him contained, and once Creed cuffed him he's compelled to obey Creed's commands."

"Has Creed commanded him to tell the truth."

"I'm not sure. Creed doesn't want me involved in the interrogation."

"Why not? Does he not know..."

Cutting Naomi off, I clarify. "He knows I have the ability to wield magic. It's just that my..."

"Heat has started up again." Naomi finishes.

"Yes."

"How are you?" Naomi asks, her concern for my wellbeing evident in her tone.

Something in my heart compels me to tell Naomi the truth, to share my secrets with the woman who has been like a mother to me.

"Creed is my fated mate, and he's also Logan and Lorelei's father." My words flow easily once I decide I'm tired of hiding behind fear and mistrust. "I was running away from my clan when I arrived in Westwood pregnant with the twins. However, before that I was in heat and somehow, I stumbled upon Creed's cabin. And I, you know, I..." Stammering, I'm relieved when Naomi puts me out of my misery.

"I understand, you shared your heat with him."

"Yes, and without meaning to we triggered our mate bond."

"But that didn't stop you from leaving him." Naomi surmises.

"No it didn't, because we didn't consummate our mate bond."

"Now you're in heat again, and Creed is your fated mate. So have the two of you consummated your mate bond?"

"Yes, we have."

An uncomfortable silence hangs between us for what seems like a lifetime before Naomi speaks.

"Rylie, answer me this, is Creed an alpha?"

"Yes, by birthright he's an alpha, but he's not leading his clan, his uncle is alpha of the Timber Valley clan."

"That doesn't matter. Your magic is directly linked to an alpha-omega bond. Which means, as long as your fated mate is a true alpha your ability to wield magic will continue to grow."

"Can Creed also be taught to wield magic?"

"I'm afraid not, Creed may be a true alpha, but he's not a Sheridan Springs true alpha."

Sheridan Springs hasn't had a true alpha in three generations. They've been made courtesy of the Council of Elders and their alpha challenges and omega breeding laws. I don't bother telling Naomi that. Understanding that my ability to wield magic actually comes from a true alpha-omega bond, I get back to why I called.

"How can I get Stryker to talk? I'm afraid we're running out of time, and we'll never get Lorelei back."

"You've already spelled the cuffs, now think of them like Wonder Woman's lasso. With you asking the questions he won't be able to lie to you."

"But he's not talking, and I know Creed isn't using gentle persuasion tactics on him."

"Stryker will answer your questions, Rylie. Remember to ask question that go beyond yes, or no. Be intentional with gaining the information you need to find Lorelei."

"Thank you, Naomi."

"I'm here for you anytime."

"Will you give Logan a kiss from me."

"You know I will."

Ending the call, I make a choice I know will piss Creed off. But first I have to wake Tess to get pass Wade.

• • • •

IT TAKES ME ALL OF two minutes to persuade Tess to distract Wade. Once she convinces him I'm upstairs sleeping, he follows his fated mate into the house eagerly. With Wade away from the door my path is clear. Stepping out onto the porch, I race down the steps and across the yard to the barn.

The sound of heavy footfalls chase after me, but I ignore Kurt's advancing frustrated growls.

Entering the barn, I shut the large door behind me before chanting a few words to keep everyone else out. With all entries to the barn spelled, Kurt's attempts to follow me inside fails. A growl I recognize as Creed losing control of his bear has me turning to face the angry glare of my mate, and the sinister grin of his captive. Although I truly believe my mate's bear will never hurt me, I'm not sure the same can be said for what his bear will do to Stryker to protect me. Unfortunately, I didn't really give myself time to hash out the details. All I know is we need answers. Now.

"I can get answers, but I need you to trust me."

The dark mocha brown eyes of Creed's bear stares down at me, and I step forward, extending my hand to my fated mate. To my utter relief he grabs hold of it, pulling me into his arms.

"I can make him talk," I murmur against Creed's pounding chest.

Nodding, Creed releases me, and we face Stryker together, united in our goal to get our daughter back by any means necessary.

When I take another step towards Stryker, Creed places his large hand on my shoulder, silently telling me that's close enough.

"What do you think you can do to get me to talk, omega?"

"You may call me Wonder Woman," I joke halfheartedly. "And you will talk."

Remembering what Naomi said about intention, I ask the most important question of all.

"Is my daughter still alive?"

"Yes," he blurts out as if unable to contain the word any longer.

Relief floods my veins, pumping blood rapidly to my heart mending it slowly. Creed's hand on my shoulder squeezes gently encouraging me to continue.

"Where have you taken my daughter?"

"I don't know where she is. She was moved yesterday."

"Why was she moved, what happened to her?" I ask frantically.

"I had her moved, when I realize you had tracked me here."

"How did you know I'd tracked you?"

"Omegas have a distinct scent, especially when they're in heat. That's how I knew you were here in Timber Valley."

"Did someone from the Sheridan Springs clan hire you to kidnap me?"

"All my contracts are anonymous."

"If your contract was for me, why did you take my little girl."

"Although most buyers want an omega for breeding immediately, there are others, whose tastes are very singular. These are the buyers who don't mind incurring the expense of keeping an underaged omega until she's ready to breed."

Bile rise in my throat, as Stryker's perverse innuendo plays on a loop in my head. Pushing down the sickness, I advance towards him before Creed has a chance to stop me. My claws extend and I lash his face before I realize what's happening. Blood soaks my palm and spatters my T-shirt, but I haven't made him bleed nearly enough.

"You can't get him to talk if he's dead."

Creed, who has now become the voice of reason, stops me from spilling more of the monster's blood.

I don't recognize my own voice when I growl, "No, but I know someone who can. So dead or alive, Stryker, you will tell us what you know about who has my daughter."

"All I know is that there's a monthly auction of shifters."

My blood boils at the thought of my little girl being auctioned to the highest bidder or worst a child molester. And my heartbreaks for the forgotten shifters no one is looking for.

"When is the next auction, and where is it held?"

"You've got about eighteen hours until the next auction. Good luck with finding it on the dark web," Stryker laughs maniacally.

"What's the web address," I ask undeterred by his cruelty.

"I don't know, you have to be invited to participate."

"Ask him where he held her before she was moved."

Like me, Creed doesn't say our daughter's name. There's no need to attempt to humanize a monster. It's just not possible.

"Answer him," I command.

"The old, abandoned power plant about twenty-miles south of Chesties."

Stryker answers Creed's question albeit unwillingly before spewing his venom.

"Omegas are no good if their already mated. Especially if their mated to an alpha. And I can smell you all over each other. But I can tell your omega is good for something other than breeding. I wonder what she'd fetch at the auction along with the kid."

"Speak again, and you won't live to find out," Creed roars menacingly.

When a risky idea occurs to me, I don't have time to run it pass Creed. Instead, I whisper an incantation to put Creed and Stryker to sleep. The barn falls silent as both shifters slumber while I gather what I hope will be helpful for my next spell. After yanking a few strands of hair from Stryker's head, I resume my place next to Creed before waking them.

Creed eyes me suspiciously, but he keeps his thoughts to himself, which I appreciate. Turning away from the scrutiny lurking in my mate's gaze, I lift the spell keeping a persistent Kurt out of the barn. When he comes barreling through the door seconds later, I hunch my shoulders as I walk pass him.

Now that we have a lead, I'm anxious to check it out. I don't bother looking back, I know Creed will follow me. He has questions only I can answer.

"Don't let him out of your sight." Creed issues the order to Kurt, closing the barn door as he exits.

"We should go check out that power plant," I suggest, aware that a closed door won't prevent Stryker from hearing us.

"Not until you've cleaned up," Creed says, taking me by the hand.

We enter the house hand-in-hand, but the unspoken words between us has put an awkward strain on our connection. Behind the closed door of Creed's bedroom, he releases my hand as if he couldn't bear to touch me any longer. Knowing he deserves an explanation; I reach for him. My heart breaks when he turns away, denying me his touch. Hurt and a little angry, I watch him disappear behind a door I assume is a closet until I hear the sound of running water. I waited for Creed to invite me to join him in the shower, but the invitation never came.

When he re-enters the bedroom ten minutes later, the towel barely covering the lower half of his body does little to hide his engorged cock. The sight of him is beyond enticing, and the thought of him filling me causes my traitorous core to ignite with desperate need.

Ignoring my body's instinct to share my heat with my fated mate, I escape to the bathroom. Frantically, I strip off the soiled clothes before stepping into the shower. Unfortunately, the spray of hot water offers no relief from the tension building in my core.

I don't know how long it takes for me to quell the heat threatening to consume me, I only know it's a matter of time before I combust.

"I got these from Tess, they should fit you," Creed says, pointing to the jeans and T-shirt laid out on the bed.

"Thank you," I reply.

Giving him my back, I drop the towel intending to dress quickly.

"I'll wait for you downstairs," Creed groans before I hear the door closing.

Left alone, my bear chooses this moment to make an appearance. Attuned to my anger, pain and frustration, my grizzly's primal instincts to protect her cubs has me racing to the bathroom. Sniffing my discarded T-shirt, the scent of Stryker's blood provides fuel for my rage, releasing my bear from her cage. I barely manage to leap out of the bedroom window before fully shifting.

Driven solely by the hunt, my bear races pass the barn, beyond our mate's treehouse and deep into the forest, allowing the scent of Stryker's blood to guide us.

Chapter 14
Creed

PUTTING SOME DISTANCE between myself and Rylie is tearing my soul in two, but it's the only way I can handle the betrayal I feel. Although I understand why she broke her promise to stay inside the house, I must admit she succeeded in getting Stryker to talk when I failed to. However, when I felt her attempt to use her magic on me, it took everything in me to resist it. Instead of falling asleep like Stryker had, I was rendered immobile, but fully aware of Rylie's deception.

When a loud disturbance outside draws my attention, long quick strides carry me to the source, my cousin Kurt. Immediately, his disheveled appearance tells me I'm not going to like what he has to say. Stalking towards me, I stand my ground as I watch him rein in his bear.

"That sonofabitch escaped," Kurt spat venomously. "One minute he's just sitting, and the next as if he knew he could break free he shifted and bolted from the barn."

The moment I realize that something must have happen to Rylie to break her spell, I'm racing back to the house. Bursting into my bedroom, I find the window opened and Rylie gone.

"Fuck fuck fuck!" I roar.

Approaching me cautiously, a visibly upset Jess asks. "Where's Rylie?"

"I don't know," I snap, taking my frustration out on my concerned sister. "Stay inside, I'll find her," I add, stepping quickly pass her.

Kurt and Wade are waiting on the porch when I instruct Jess once again to stay inside before pulling the front door shut.

"What can I do to help," Wade offers.

"Take care of my sisters and your cubs."

Nodding, Wade enters the house, and I turn to Kurt. "Track Stryker down, bring him back or kill him, I don't care which."

My cousin's toothy grin appears more wolfish than bear. Knowing I have the right shifter for the job, I make my way to my truck.

"And where are you going?" Kurt asks.

"To bring my mate back home."

Climbing behind the wheel of my Silverado, my destination is clear, the old, abandoned power plant twenty-miles south of Chesties, that's where I'll find Rylie.

• • • •

AS MY BOOTS HIT THE ground of the rundown parking lot of the old power plant, my mate's scent lingers in the morning breeze around me. Following her scent to where it's strongest, I enter the building in search of her.

I didn't know what to expect once I found her, but finding her naked hadn't entered my mind. Unfortunately, her words forces the image of her naked body from my mind. Listening to a one-sided conversation, my heartbreaks when I hear the hopelessness in my mate's voice.

"I'll do anything, just give me back my little girl," she pleas. "Take me instead, I'm the one you want."

A moment of silence goes by, and I assume she's listening to the person on the other end of the call.

"How do I sever my mate bond?" She whimpers into the phone.

I can't believe Rylie would even consider severing our mate bond. However, if it meant getting Lorelei back, it would destroy my soul, but I would let my mate go to save our daughter.

"You want me to choose between my fated mate and my little girl?"

As if finally scenting me, Rylie turns to face me. Seeing her tears flow unrestrained, I close the distance between us.

"I can get our daughter back, but I need you to trust me." I plea, repeating a variation of her words. "Please consider what happens if you turn yourself over to these bastards and they keep Lorelei. Logan and I would lose you both. I promise you I'll get our daughter back. I promise you will hold our little girl in your arms again."

Holding her chest, she cries. "It hurts. It hurts so much."

Attempting to console my heartbroken mate, I pull Rylie into my arms as the phone drops to the floor.

"I know," I croon, stroking her back as her tears soaked my shirt.

"I'm sorry," she murmurs through muffled cries.

"Forgiven," I reply because I knew deep in my heart I had already forgiven her betrayal. A betrayal brought on by a mother's desperation.

Releasing Rylie, I give her the shirt off my back to cover her naked body. When indistinguishable chatter from the discarded phone draws my attention I reach down to pick it up. Placing the cell phone on speaker, I address the listener.

"You will regret taking my cub. You will regret the pain you have caused my mate."

For a few seconds I can hear the listener's harsh breathing before the call ends. Shoving the cell phone in my back pocket, I take Rylie by the hand.

"Let's take a look around," I say, needing to do something useful.

Agreeing, Rylie and I inspect the power plant from top to bottom leaving no corner of the building undisturbed. When we find nothing helpful, I feel my mate's disappointment through our mate bond. It's not until we reach the lowest level of the power plant that a faint clanking sound reach our ears.

"Did you hear that?" Rylie asks.

"I did. It's coming from there," I say, pointing to the door that reads boiler room.

Listening closely, I hear the sound of multiple heartbeats. When Rylie's eyes widen with shock and fear, I know she hears them too. Putting Rylie's safety first, I motion for her to step behind me. I'm grateful when all she does is protest with a pout before following in step behind me.

Pushing open the metal door of the boiler room, I enter the dark space ahead of Rylie. I'm immediately assaulted by the odious stench of bodily fluids, and the smell of the rusty remnants of unused equipment long forgotten. The clank becomes louder, and I follow the sound to four females shifters cowering together in a cage. Thoughtfully, I approach the cage so as not to frightened the females, but that doesn't stop them from scurrying away.

Stepping out from behind me, Rylie gasps when she sees the state of the females, barely clothed, no shoes and trapped in a filthy cage that looks more like a heavy-duty kennel.

"We won't hurt you," she says, taking tentative strides toward the caged females. "I'm Rylie and this is Creed, my mate. We're looking for our daughter. She was kidnapped three days ago. We have reason to believe she was held here. Have any of you seen her? She's three years old, with blonde hair and blue eyes."

They remain quiet for long seconds before one of the females step forward, a shifter of African American descent with a crown of braids, and a unique scent I don't recognize. Unlike the others she's not an omega.

"Release us, and I'll tell you what I know."

Moving to stand next to Rylie, I ask. "You're all shifters, why haven't you freed yourselves?"

"We've tried."

Understanding that magic is holding them captive, I turn to Rylie.

"Can you free them?"

"I can try."

Grabbing hold of the bars, Rylie begins chanting and the females step back. I observe my mate attempt to free the shifters but fail to break the spell holding them captive.

"My magic isn't strong enough to get pass whatever spell was used to keep them caged," Rylie concludes.

"What can I do to help?"

Reaching for my hand, she says, "Our mate bond is the source of my magic. So maybe a physical connection will give it a boost."

Taking hold of Rylie's hand, I instinctively place my free hand on the cage. Rylie starts to chant once again, and I feel the warmth of her magic flowing between us. When she releases the bar of the cage abruptly, I do as well.

"What is it?" I ask. "Why did you stop?"

Showing me the palms of her hands, she says. "It burns."

"We'll find another way," I assure the females staring at us with defeat in their weary eyes.

"Please try again."

The female with the braided crown begs. Extending her hands palm up through the bars, she offers her hands to Rylie.

"Take my hands and try again. Please."

Sensing there's more to this shifter than meets the eye, I issue a warning.

"If you hurt my mate this cage will be the least of your worries."

"I only want to help her to free us."

Nodding, I step aside as Rylie takes the female shifter's hands. A soft white light glows between their joined palm before she releases Rylie's hands.

"Please try again," she repeats.

Facing the cage, Rylie takes hold of two bars, one in each hand. I place my right hand over her left before grabbing hold of a third bar with my free hand once again. As Rylie's chant becomes louder, the bars beneath our hands begin to shake. One by one the bars dissolve in our hands, leaving the space wide enough for the females to step through.

"We did it," Rylie cheers.

Holding both her hands in mine, I turn them palm side up to check for the redness. To my relief her palms weren't burnt.

"You have your freedom, now tell us what you know about our daughter."

Nodding, the female doesn't appear to take offense at my tone, but I can tell she doesn't appreciate it.

"Anything you can tell us might be helpful," Rylie adds.

"The little girl you described was here with the rest of us until yesterday," she says, confirming what Stryker has already told us.

Retrieving my cell phone from my back pocket, I show her a photo of Lorelei.

"Is this her? Is this the little girl?"

Staring at the photo of Lorelei, she nods. "That's her."

Rylie reaches out to her and like a skittish pup, she jumps back.

"I'm sorry," Rylie says, placing her hands back down at her sides. "I didn't mean to frighten you."

"Your daughter wasn't harmed while she was here. We looked after her the best we could under the circumstances."

"Thank you," Rylie chokes out.

"How long have you been here?" I ask.

"Nearly four weeks, but the others have been here longer."

"We'll make sure you all get back to your families," Rylie assures them.

"We don't have families to get back to." A petite shifter with sandy brown hair who has remained quiet until now, whispers meekly.

"We'll help you however we can," Rylie amends. "For now let's get out of this place."

Leading the way, Rylie and I escort the females to the parking lot. They climb into the back of my pickup, one after the other eager for freedom. I take them to the safest place I know, the Masterson family homestead.

Frank is there to greet us when we arrive, and the concerned look he gives me when he sees the four females proves I made the right choice.

"They need our help," Rylie explains, before Frank or I have a chance to exchange words.

"Tess, Jess." Frank calls out to my sisters.

Jess steps out onto the porch, coming to an abrupt stop when she sees Rylie and the four female shifters.

Bounding down the steps, she gives Rylie a hug before asking. "What can I do to help?"

"We need to get them cleaned up and fed." Rylie responds emphatically.

"Come with me, please," Jess urges.

The females turn to Rylie, who gives them a subtle nod and they follow Jess. As they enter the house two-by-two holding hands, I hear my mate breathe a sigh of relief.

"I should get cleaned up as well," she says.

With less than fifteen hours until the auction, I don't have time to take a break if I intend to keep my promise to Rylie and bring our daughter back home where she belongs.

"I have a few calls to make before we speak with the females again."

Nodding, Rylie excuses herself, leaving me alone with Frank.

"What have you found out?" Frank asks leading me away from the house.

"There's an auction on the dark web at midnight, but we have no way of accessing it."

"Your mate has access to magic I'm not going to pretend to understand, but maybe there's some sort of spell that can help."

Recalling how Rylie had burned her hands attempting to free the females, I can't stand the thought of her pain. I'm ready to dismiss the idea when Rylie's words gives me other options.

"No, but I know someone who can. So dead or alive, Stryker, you will tell us what you know about who has my daughter."

Rylie knows two powerful witches, one more powerful than the other. Witches who has helped her with her magic from the beginning, so maybe now they will help us get our daughter back. Turning back towards the house, I take off in a sprint.

"Magic may just be the answer," I call out over my shoulder to Frank.

Chapter 15
Rylie

WITH JESS AND TESS, seeing to the care of the female shifters Creed and I freed from a cage in the abandoned power plant, I look after my own needs. Stepping under the shower for the second time this morning, I try to force the sound of a ticking clock from my head. Unfortunately, nothing I do stops the passing of time. The seconds and minutes continues to count down my little girl's fate.

Returning to the bedroom after a quick shower, the jeans and T-shirt Creed borrowed from Tess is still on the bed where I left them. I'm pulling the T-shirt over my head when Creed enters the bedroom. For a moment, I want to give in to my heat, and forget my aching heart. But it isn't easy to forget the reason my heart beats. My cubs and my mate are my reasons.

"We need the Westwood pack's help," Creed says without preamble.

"What can they do we haven't already done?"

"Magic. They have powerful magic, and that's what we need to get Lorelei back."

Retrieving a cell phone from his pocket, I recognize it as the phone I found in the power plant.

"Here me out," he says, taking a seat on the bed.

"Go on, I'm listening."

Wordlessly, Creed waits for me to take a seat next to him. Giving him my full attention, I sit down.

"We have this cell phone, which I assume belongs to Stryker, we have his blood, and you have strands of his hair."

Unable to conceal the telltale signs of my guilt, I lower my head attempting to hide the rapid blinking of my lashes.

"I can explain," I offer lamely.

"I assume you intended to use it to track him somehow."

Nodding, I meet my mate's gaze when he lifts my chin. Although I expect to find distrust, all I see is hope twinkling in his moonlit eyes.

"I wanted to track where he'd been, since we had him captive at the time I assume he wouldn't be going anywhere anytime soon."

"That's a great idea, but we still need the Westwood pack to help us because we're running out of time."

"Okay," I agree. "I'll give Naomi a call."

Reaching for my cell phone on the bedside table, I begin to call Naomi, but Creed stops me.

"We don't have time for a go between. We need to go directly to the source. We need to call Calian Westwood, the pack's alpha."

Understanding the hierarchy of the Westwood pack as I do my own clan, I call Calian. However, I didn't expect him to answer on the first ring, but I'm truly grateful he did.

"Hello, Rylie. I've been expecting your call. What can I do for you?"

Returning his greeting, it takes me a few minutes to catch him up on our progress before I get to why I called.

"We have less than fifteen hours to get Lorelei back. We don't know where she's being held, but I'm hopeful Aria and Naomi can locate her before the auction starts."

Tears cloud my eyes, and my throat constricts with the realization that this may be our only chance at saving our little girl. Pulling me into his arms, Creed finishes for me.

"Even with Aria and Naomi's help, we need a backup plan," Creed says without preamble. "We need someone who has the financial means to enter the auction and bid to win. I can sell my family's homestead and withdraw everything from my bank accounts, and it wouldn't be enough. But if you do this for us I'll spend the rest of my life repaying you if that's what it takes to get our daughter back."

"I've been aware that Lorelei and Logan are your cubs since the day we met." Calian confesses. "But it wasn't my secret to share."

"I understand, and I thank you for keeping my son safe," Creed says graciously. "Will you help me get my daughter back."

"Where are you?" Calian asks.

"We're at my family's homestead in Timber Valley Utah," Creed replies. "I've just sent you the exact location."

"There's a private airstrip one hundred miles north of your location. I can have a Westwood jet there in ninety minutes."

"We'll be there," Creed confirms. "Thank you, Westwood."

"You can thank me after we get your daughter back," Calian says.

Ending the call, Creed and I make our way downstairs to say goodbye to his family for now. We're standing on the porch when Jess tells us one of the female shifters left. Without being told I know it's the shifter that healed my burned palms. Realizing she never told us her name, I decide to refer to her as *Queen*, for the crown of braided hair atop her head.

• • • •

ITS LUNCHTIME WHEN we reach the Westwood estate, but I can't be bother with food when seeing my moonbeam again is all the nourishment my soul needs. Scooping him up into my arms, I pepper his cherub cheeks with all the kisses I've missed giving him over the past three days. When his little arms hug me back, I never want to let him go.

"Mommy, did you get Lori back from the monster?"

"Not yet, Moonbeam."

Desperately wanting to give my son something positive to focus on, I look to Creed for the answer. Silently I mouth. "*Would you like to meet your son?*"

Joyous eyes that mirrors our son's smile back at me as Creed nods yes. Taking a seat with Logan still in my arms, I turn him on my lap to face his father.

"Moonbeam, I have someone I'd like you to meet."

Staring up at Creed, he says. "My eyes are gray too, that's why my mommy calls me Moonbeam."

"My father had gray eyes too," Creed shares.

Hopping down off my lap, Logan stands between me and his father. I watch as my son turns from Creed to me and back to his father before asking. "Are you my father?"

Tears prick the corners of my eyes when Creed drops to his knees before our son and extend his hand.

"Yes, I'm your father, and it's so good to meet you, son."

My heart burst with unimaginable joy when Logan places his little hand onto Creed's palm.

"It's good to meet you too..."

As if sensing Logan is unsure what to say next, Creed provides our son with an option.

"For now you may call me Creed. But someday soon I hope you'll call me dad."

Nodding, Logan accepts Creed's offer.

"Moonbeam, I need to talk to Omi and Aria, will you be my big boy and show your dad your favorite place to play."

Smiling broadly, Logan tugs on Creed's hand urging him to stand. My mate towers over our son like a looming mountain before he lifts Logan up onto his shoulders. Giggling, Logan points to the door.

"Let's go find Kota."

"Who's Kota?" Creed asks.

"My best friend."

"Dakota Westwood, he's Aria and Calian's son," I clarify.

"He has three dads," Logan adds.

"Is that so?" Creed questions.

"But my dad is a hero."

Logan response catches both Creed and I off guard and we look to our son questioningly.

"Because my dad is going to get Lori back so we can be a family."

I'm too emotional to respond when Logan's gleeful declaration punches me in the gut.

"Okay, then let's go find Kota," Creed says tactfully.

Bending to give me a kiss, Creed's lips smile against mine briefly, before stooping lower for Logan to do the same.

"I'll see you soon," my mate announces with our giggling son high atop his shoulders.

• • • •

THE GATHERING OF THE witches takes place in the forest. Aria says, earth is the element we will draw upon to find Stryker. Since most shifter's thrive in nature, it stands to reason that Aria, being both witch and wolf will tap into the element the witch-wolf hybrid shares.

Creating a locator spell with the items provided, Naomi extracts Stryker's blood from my T-shirt. I watch fascinated as each drop of blood trickles into a stone mortar. And when she drops in Stryker's strands of hair, she gives the mortar and pestle to me.

"This is your spell, Rylie. Aria and I are simply here to aid you."

Confused, I blurt out. "But my magic isn't powerful enough."

"Not yet," Aria says. "But your love for Lorelei is. We can create the spell, but the intention and the words must come from you."

Accepting my daughter's fate has always been in my hands, I begin grinding the blood and hair until it's the consistency of a fine paste.

"Very good," Naomi says, after viewing the contents of the mortar. "Now it's time for you to create your salt circle. It will protect you while you're casting your spell.

Shoving a clear crystal into each of the front pockets of my jeans, I begin drawing the salt circle on the floor of the forest, placing four bundles of sage and lighting them clockwise on the circle for protection. Once the salt circle is complete, Naomi and Aria observe my creation with encouraging smiles.

"Did you bring the other items as well?" Aria asks.

Reaching into my tote bag, I retrieve Lorelei's teddy bear and Stryker's cell phone. According to Aria, Lorelei's teddy bear will focus my intention, and Stryker's phone is needed for the communication spell.

"You will need this as well," Naomi says, offering me a small circular mirror. "So you can see what Stryker sees."

Stepping into the center of the salt circle, I place the mirror on the ground, trace a circle along the mirror using the paste from the mortar before sitting Stryker's cellphone atop the mirror. Aria and Naomi give me a nod of support and encouragement as I take a seat at the center of the salt circle on the forest floor. Holding Lorelei's teddy bear close to my chest, I chant the words to the protection spell I learned from Aria. *Provide me protection from all that seek to harm me.* After repeating the incantation three times as Aria instructed, I call out to Stryker mentally.

Slowly a distorted image of the monster appears in the mirror. Squeezing Lorelei's teddy tight, I focus on getting my daughter back. I focus on the day, Creed, Logan, Lorelei and I are finally a family. Tuning out the sounds of the forest, I push my gift farther than I ever have. Suddenly, the magic of the alpha-omega bond I share with my fated mate answers my call for help.

When the mirror image of Stryker becomes clear, I take in his surroundings. Unfortunately, after examining every aspect of the image, I find nothing helpful. It's not until I'm ready to beg Naomi and Aria for help that a new spell echoes in my mind. Chanting the words to the spell, I force my way into

Stryker's subconscious. Careful to hide my presence, I try to think like him.

"So what do you think I'll get for the omega cub?"

"Not as much as her mother, but I'm sure the bidders won't disappoint you."

Hearing a female's voice respond, I try to identify her. Willing Stryker to look at her, I get a glimpse of a much older woman whose body appears disfigured by age. When he turns away from her abruptly, I get the feeling he's not permitted to look upon this woman.

Desperate for Lorelei's location, I push the question into Stryker's head.

"So where is the cub now?"

"With the others awaiting the auction."

"I'd like to watch the auction."

A long unbearable silent falls between Stryker and the old woman, and I pray to the gods that I didn't push too hard for answers.

"*You've never wanted to watch before."* The old woman says *after a few long seconds.*

"Never had a reason to before. Besides, this is my first cub in the auction. If it sells well, I know where I can get more."

"Very well, you may watch. I'll send the link to your phone."

My heart begins pounding erratically, realizing that Stryker may have already replaced his phone. Fortunately, seconds later, Stryker retrieves his cell phone from his pocket. When he opens a text message, I practically shout my thanks to the gods when the screen of his cell phone with a view of the link reflects in the mirror. Quickly memorizing the authorization to access the auction, I jump out of Stryker's mind before stepping out of the salt circle to text the information to Creed.

This is how you access the auction. I'm going to continue to track Stryker.

Sending off the text to Creed, I step back into the center of the salt circle.

Chapter 16
Creed

AFTER SPENDING A COUPLE of hours getting to know my son, I regret having to leave him. Although our separation is temporary, his attempt at trying to hide his disappointment still breaks my heart.

"I'll be back before you know it, son."

"Will you tuck me in like Kota's dad."

"I'll be back to tuck you in. I promise."

"Okay," Logan smiles, but it doesn't reach his eyes.

Hoping to build trust between myself and my son, I silently vow to tuck him in tonight and every night until he tells me to stop. For now it's my daughter who needs me. After receiving a text from Rylie, I know it's time to initiate our backup plan. Leaving Logan to play with his friend, Dakota, under the watchful supervision of Rosalie, I seek out Calian.

When I reach his home office, the door is open, so I walk in. Finding him sitting at his desk, with his laptop open, I clear my throat to gain his attention.

"We have the authorization to access the auction," I announce.

"That's great, let's get started," Westwood replies.

Handing over my cell phone with the text message from Rylie on the screen, I wait impatiently for a sign from Westwood that he's gain access to the auction.

"Have a seat, Masterson." Now that we know where to look, I still need an invitation to enter the bidding."

"What do you mean," I growl in frustration.

"This only gives me access to view the auction."

"So how the fuck do you get an invitation to bid?"

Ignoring my outburst, Westwood says, "I've sent an offer the auction host won't be able to refuse."

"And how long will that take?"

"I can't say, it could take a few minutes, or the host could drag it out until the start of the auction."

"Fuck!"

"In the meantime, I'll stay in the chat group with the other viewers and bidders to gain whatever information I can about where Lorelei is being held."

Nodding my understanding, the helplessness I feel has me striding over to Westwood's mini bar. Although I'm fully aware that alcohol doesn't affect shifters in the same way it does humans, I pour myself two fingers of Pappy Van Winkle's Family Reserve regardless. Lifting the tumbler to my lips, the sweet scents of chocolate and caramel fill my nostrils. As I toss down the alcohol in one big gulp the woodsy flavor coats my tongue, followed by a rush of heat sliding down my throat. When the warmth of bourbon hits my belly, I'm reminded that I haven't eaten since my picnic dinner in my cabin with Rylie last night.

For the next several hours, I pace Westwood's office wearing the rug beneath my feet thin. Until Rylie comes running into the office with Naomi and Aria close behind her.

"I know where Stryker is!" Rylie shouts.

Quick hopeful strides carry me to her side in an instant, and before I ask she blurts out.

"He's in Chesterfield."

"How do you know he's in Chesterfield?"

"I recognize the diner. It's the same diner..."

"Where you first saw him?"

"Yes," she nods.

With time being against us, I ask Westwood for another favor. Vowing to somehow repay him for his kindness and generosity, I step to him, father to father and alpha to alpha.

"How fast can that jet of yours get me to Chesterfield?"

"It's a thirty-minute ride to the Westwood private airstrip. So save yourself some time and take the helicopter, it'll get you there quicker. The helicopter is on the estate." Westwood says, answering my unspoken question. Lifting his cell phone from the desk, he adds. "I would fly you myself, but..."

Cutting him off, I inform him it's not necessary. "I can pilot the helicopter myself."

"Alright, ask Rosalie for the key and she'll direct you to the helipad."

Nodding my thanks, I take Rylie by the hand leading her out of the office. In the kitchen we find Rosalie with Logan and Dakota. Logan's eyes beam with joy when he sees his mother and I enter the kitchen. When he stands from the table, racing towards us, I scoop him up into my arms. While taking a few moments to hold my son, I notice Rylie has retrieved the key from Rosalie.

"Want me to show you my favorite pony?"

"Maybe later, son. I have to run a quick errand first."

"Can I go with you?"

"Not this time, son."

"Okay."

I'm quickly learning when my son says okay, he's anything but. Fortunately, my mate has a way of soothing our cub, I've yet to learn.

"Logan, you and I will stay here with Kota and Omi until daddy gets back. But we can go watch him fly away in the helicopter."

A pair of twinkling silvery gray eyes that match my own beams with excitement, and I get caught up in the joys of fatherhood and what it will be like to teach my cubs what it truly means to be a bear shifter.

"When I get back, I'll take you up for a few minutes,"

Giving me a hug so tight, my son whispers. "Okay, daddy."

Hugging him back, I fight against the tears threatening to fall.

"We should get going," Rylie says.

It takes us a few minutes to reach the helipad, but once it's in sight Logan sprints ahead of his mother and me to see it up close. Reaching the helicopter I do a quick assessment of the exterior before lifting Logan up into the cockpit.

"I need my co-pilot to help me with the preflight check of the cockpit before I take off. Can you do that for me, son?"

Smiling gleefully, Logan says. "I can do that, daddy."

"First we need to put these on," I say covering his ears with an aviation headset. After taking the pilot's seat, I cover my own ears. "Next we make sure everything is working the way its suppose to before I take off."

"Preflight check," Logan says eagerly.

"That's right," I confirm proudly.

With Rylie looking on, Logan and I finish up and I'm ready to take flight.

"You're an excellent co-pilot, son. You'll be flying before you know it."

"Daddy..."

Logan calls out but doesn't continue.

"Yes, son."

"Will you teach me how to fly a helicopter like you?"

"Yes, I will, but first I have to run my errand so I can get back in time to tuck you in." Removing the aviation headsets from my head and then Logan's, I climb out of the cockpit. "For now I need you to look after mommy while I'm away."

Hopping out the co-pilot's seat, my son races to my mate. Rylie lifts Logan up into her arms, watching me approach them.

"I'll be back as soon as I can," I say, holding them both in my arms.

Rylie tilts her chin up to me, offering me her mouth. While Logan rests his head on his mother's shoulder facing away from us. Grateful for my son's innocent act of discretion, I kiss my mate deeply for long heart-stopping dick-throbbing seconds until she pulls away.

"Hurry back to us," she whispers against my lips.

Turning quickly on my heels, I race back to the helicopter. From the cockpit I wave to Rylie and Logan, as the helicopter ascends smoothly. I hover in the sky above them until they were safely under the roof of the Westwood estate.

· · · ·

LANDING THE HELICOPTER in the parking lot of a Walmart a few blocks from the diner, I proceed on foot. When I enter the diner, I expect Stryker to be long gone, and he is.

Fortunately, he hasn't been gone long, his scent is still strong enough for me to track. With my heighten sense of smell, I focus on isolating Stryker's scent, and it doesn't take me long to figure out he's not alone. A second scent, female, seems to mirror his movements onto the streets. After tracking Stryker and his companion to a shifter caravan park deep in the forest, I announce my arrival.

"Stryker!"

Aware there's a stranger among them, my voice echoing is the only sound the forest makes, until the sound of birds taking flight and rodents scurrying for safety reaches my ears. The door to a caravan opens, revealing an old woman. Recognizing her scent, I walk in the direction of her caravan.

"There's no Stryker here," she lies unconvincingly.

"Yet, I've tracked him to this very spot."

"We don't want any trouble," she says feebly, and somehow I know it's all just an act.

Deciding to speak my truth I lay my cards on the table.

"Stryker has kidnapped my cub, and he intends to sell her during a shifter auction at midnight." A few shifters step out of their caravans, and I continue. "Unless any of you intend to try to stop me, I will find him."

"We're not a pack." A female wolf shifter speaks up. "But this forest is our home, and we try to look out for each other when we can."

"I know most of you are wolf shifters, so I know you can scent that I'm a bear shifter. So is Stryker. Turning back to the old woman I add. "And he has been traveling with her as recent as a few hours ago."

"You will leave us in peace." The old woman says with more force this time.

When she begins to chant, I recognize her for what she truly is. A witch with fading magic. Spreading her fingers wide as if to draw magic into her body, her efforts fail when all she manages to do is rustle the leaves of a few trees.

"I'm not here for you, witch."

"The bear shifter you seek is out hunting." The female wolf shifter says before stepping back into her caravan.

Following the scent of a fresh kill, I find Stryker easily. With a large buck across his shoulders and the blood of the dead animal coating his bare chest, my bear asserts his dominance with a menacing growl. Animal instincts take over and my bear is set free. Racing towards the beast wearing human skin, my bear charges Stryker, knocking him to the ground.

Seconds later, fully shifted we're locked in a battle for dominance, biting and clawing with the intend to kill. Stryker's bear manage to escape the fury of my bear's claws by biting into my bear's chest. Lost to the will of an uncaged animal, my mind gives way to my bear's need to survive at all cost.

When my bear's massive claw rips into the face of Stryker's, we watch him fall to the ground in defeat. His ferocious growls fills the air before slowly fading to whimpering roars of pain as he shifts back to his human skin.

Relinquishing control back to me, the sound of my bear's vicious growls startle the inhabitants of the forest. After shifting back, I'm grateful when I'm fully clothed moments later curtesy of my mate's spell.

With Stryker bleeding out and near death, I head out of the forest eager to get back to my family. It's not until I've taken a few steps that I notice my fist clenched tightly. Unfurling my bloody fingers, I discover a detached lifeless eye in the palm of my hand. I suppress the urge to keep it as a trophy. Instead, I toss it into the forest to feed whatever creature that happens to find it.

The sun is setting by the time I make it back to the nomadic shifters caravan park. Although I didn't intend to stop, the female wolf shifter urge me to do so.

"I know you're in a hurry, but may I have a moment of your time?"

"What can I do for you?" I ask with as much politeness I can muster under the circumstances.

"I overheard the witch talking to the bear shifter before you arrived," she says ignoring my bluntness. "She mentioned a midnight delivery and receiving precious cargo."

Taken by surprise, I ask. "Did she happen to say where this delivery will take place?"

"She was kinda cryptic with the bear shifter, like she was keeping it a secret from him. But I know this area, so when she mentioned a coven. I knew she was referring to the Manchester House. The house has been abandoned since the witches loss their power about four years ago. And there hasn't been an active coven since."

Scenting the air, I ask. "How long has the witch been gone?"

"She left soon after you went looking for Stryker."

"Thank you, I truly appreciate your willingness to help."

Rubbing her belly, she says. "My little one isn't even here yet, but I know I would stop at nothing to get my pup back if he was ever taken from me."

"Congratulations and thank you again."

"You don't owe me a thank you for doing the right thing. Now go find your cub."

Racing out of the forest, I reach the helicopter intending to update Rylie and the Westwood pack. Unfortunately, a dead cell phone means, I'm on my own. It also means I have to break my promise to tuck my son in tonight.

· · · ·

AFTER CONFISCATING a vehicle from the parking lot of Walmart, I make my way to Manchester House. The old Victorian house stands out in a neighborhood of modern single-family homes. Sitting atop a hill at the end of the street, it's as if the house has been there for hundreds of years and everything else grew around it or in spite of it.

Making my way up the hill, I park a few houses down and continue on foot. Once I'm over the black wrought iron gate the old gothic house appears more imposing and creepier as hell with its pointed arches and ornate carving.

Although I don't see any security cameras, I avoid taking the direct route along the intricate stone driveway leading up to the house. Using the large trees and overgrown shrubberies for cover, I do a quick sweep of the grounds. Discovering two shifters guarding the entrances, one at the front and another at the rear of the house, I quickly and quietly eliminate the obstacles preventing me from entering the house.

Once inside the house, I'm surprised how well maintain it is. The interior of the house is a shocking contrast to the exterior. But something tells me the ruse is designed to scare off nosy neighbors. After all who wants to step foot in a witch's creepy old house.

Starting on the entry level, I search one room after the other, before heading upstairs to search the bedrooms. When I find no sign of Lorelei or the old woman, I begin to lose hope of ever finding my daughter. Lost in the deepest pit of pain and despair, I walk mindlessly back to the library. Anger and frustration tempt my bear from his cage with extended claws, and I begin tearing apart the room. Even without fully shifting I possess the strength of ten men. Unable to control the rage, I tear through the room like an unstoppable cyclone.

When the bulk of my fury is spent, I survey the destruction, ripped paintings, tossed furniture and pages from books scattered everywhere. Noticing a cracked between the bookcase and the fireplace, I hurry to inspect it, because there's no fucking way there's a secret passage behind the bookcase. But I hope for it regardless.

Pulling the bookcase from the wall, my knees go week finding an opening to a dark passageway. Undeterred, I step into the darkness. Following the path toward the hint of light I see ahead; I find what can only be described as a witch's altar. A shrine to whatever deity or demon the witch worships. Throughout the musky space there are candles, incense, a jeweled chalice, and an athamé, a ceremonial blade with a black handle. I know enough about witches to know these are the tools used for most rituals.

Daring to investigate further, I discover various symbols circling the altar. And since I'm not foolish enough to step inside a witch's circle, I back away. Cautious footsteps carry me deeper into the cavernous lair of the witch before the sound of music draws my attention.

The music begins to fade as I advance towards it, replaced by the rhythm of four heartbeats. Arriving at a closed, old wooden door, fit for a dungeon, I pushed it open with a thud against the inner wall.

The sight of three females lying on cots sleeping, has me rushing recklessly into the room. Scenting the air, I discover the females are omegas. After failing to wake them from whatever spell the witch has them under, I suddenly remember I heard four heartbeats. Searching frantically, I breathe a heavy sigh of relief hearing the steady beat of a strong heart of a forth omega.

Following the thumping rhythm to a much smaller female, the sight of golden blonde hair and cherub cheeks causes my heart to pound erratically in my chest. Scenting the air once again, I confirm what every fiber of my being is telling me. This tiny female is my cub, my daughter, my Lorelei. Dropping to my knees, I look upon her for the first time. When the sight of her awakens the same fatherly instincts I feel for Logan, I know there's nothing I wouldn't do to keep her safe.

When I'm unable to wake Lorelei the sound of her steady breathing and strong heartbeat gives me a measure of comfort. Putting my cub's safety first, I lift her up into my arms before attempting to wake the females again. Unable to wake them, and fully aware I can't carry them all, I choose to save my daughter, escaping the way I came.

Chapter 17
Rylie

WITH A LITTLE LESS than an hour left until the shifter auction begins, Creed still hasn't returned from Chesterfield, the host of the auction hasn't accepted Calian's offer to allow him to enter the bidding, and Logan refuses to go to bed before his father returns to tuck him in for the night. Feeling Creed's presence through our mate bond is the only reason I'm not freaking out about him being gone so long. As long as I can feel him I know he'll come back to us.

"Don't lose hope, Rylie," Naomi says, joining me at the kitchen table.

"I won't stop until I find her," I vow.

"I know because that's what good parents do. They go above and beyond for their children." Naomi sighs longingly. "I wasn't blessed with my own child, but I raised Aria as if she where mine, and I know without a doubt I would never give up on her."

Entering the kitchen, Aria responds. "You're my mother in every way that counts."

"I never knew my mother, but you're the mother I've always dreamt of having," I share.

"Then I'm doubly bless to have two such amazing women consider me as their mother."

The three of us share a moment of silence, and I pray to the gods Lorelei and Creed return soon. As if reading my thoughts Aria asks.

"Have you heard from Creed?"

Shaking my head, I share my hope. "No, but I can still feel him through our mate bond, so I'm sure he'll return soon."

"I'm sure he will. It's clear to see how much he loves you."

Although Naomi has provided me with a temporary remedy to quell my heat in Creed's absence, I feel myself blushing red hot at the mention of his name.

"How's your pup? Do you know if you're carrying a male or female?" I ask, changing the subject.

Smiling brightly, rubbing her protruding belly bump, she coos, "This little one is male."

"That's great, another son. Cal..."

Realizing I don't know which of her mates is the biological father, I falter mid-sentence.

"It's okay to be confused by it. My mates and I share everything, including parenthood. However, biologically the pup I'm carrying is Anakin's son." Aria clarifies. "And my next son will be Kai's"

Shocked, I can't hold back the next question that blurts out. "And you already know this?"

"Nodding, Aria smiles. "I do."

Desperate for some insight into my own future, I ask. "Will I get Lorelei back?"

Taking a seat at the table, Aria takes my hands in hers. "I've seen you happy, Rylie, and I've seen you surrounded by your cubs, but I haven't been able to see their faces. So I don't know if Lorelei is among them."

"Thank you."

Releasing my hands, Aria makes her way to the refrigerator. I watch her stare into the fridge without pulling anything out.

As if her cravings manifest more than a need for food, Anakin appears at her side. I turn away from them when Aria leans into Anakin, but I hear the joy in her laughter when he picks her up and carry her from the kitchen.

"They never seem to tire," Naomi comments with a chuckle.

"I'm in awe of her. To be so powerful, and so grounded. She's amazing."

"She's..."

Naomi words die in her throat when Santana stalks into the kitchen. From the way she stares at him, I can tell from the look in Naomi's eyes her mate comes baring bad news.

"Rylie, I need you to come to Calian's office now," Santana urges.

When Santana doesn't wait for me to acknowledge him, I'm on my feet racing after him. Entering Calian's office, the grim look on his face stops me in my tracks.

"The auction is over, and the link to the auction site has expired," Calian says.

"How's that possible? It's not midnight." Pulling my cell phone from my pocket, I check the time. "There still thirty minutes before it begins."

"I'm sorry, Rylie," Calian says, but his words offer no comfort.

It's 11:30 p.m., I mutter to myself, desperate to figure out what went wrong. It's 11:30 in Westwood, but it's after midnight in Timber Valley. Questioning where I failed my daughter, I want to believe Stryker deliberately misled me. I want to believe that even under my confession spell he was able to lie to me. Facing the truth, I'm forced to accept it was just dumb fucking luck, a miscalculation of time that has stolen my last chance at getting my little girl back.

Pacing the floor, I beg the gods to reverse time and give me back my Lorelei, I plead for any manner of divine intervention that will give me back my child. When that fails, I drop to my knees in an inconsolable heap screaming as the dam breaks drowning me in hopeless despair.

I'm vaguely aware of Santana lifting me from the floor, and Naomi holding me tight as heart wrenching sobs rack my body.

• • • •

I DON'T KNOW HOW LONG I've been lying in bed holding Logan close to my heart while he sleeps peacefully in my arms. I am, however, painfully aware that as the silent tears I shed for his sister continues to decimate my soul, my desperation to hold onto him grows. Long after Santana carried me to a guest room of the Westwood estate, my only thought has been to keep my son safe.

When the sound of a helicopter reach my ears, I'm too distraught to greet Creed. I know I should seek the comfort of my mate, and offer him comfort as well, but I can't bring myself to leave Logan alone. A tap at the door, followed by Naomi peeking her head into the bedroom has me pretending to sleep.

"I know you're awake, Rylie. The shifters can hear you crying.

"Please just leave me alone."

"Creed needs your help."

A sharp spike of pain tightens my chest at the thought of losing my mate. Climbing out of bed, I'm careful not to wake Logan.

"He's in the family room," Naomi says when I open the bedroom door.

Following Naomi to the Westwood family room, I fear the worst causing heavy footsteps to slow my trek. Thankfully, Creed is at the entrance to greet me when I approach. Seeing for myself that he's unharmed, I turn a questioning glance to Naomi before she retreats in the opposite direction. I go willingly when my mate pulls me into his arm, and I respond eagerly to the deep needful kiss he gives me.

"I will always try my best to keep my promises to you," he moans against my lips.

Tears flow freely down my cheeks, recalling the promise he made to me. *I promise you I'll get our daughter back. I promise you will hold our little girl in your arms again.* The promise he wasn't able to keep.

"Some promises are beyond our control to keep," I choke out through anguished tears.

"But not this one," Creed says, leading me into the family room. "This vow was always mine to keep."

"What..."

At the sight of a little blonde bundle curled up on the couch sleeping, I forget to breathe, unable to voice the words caught in my throat.

"I found our cub, Goldie. I found Lorelei."

Rushing over to the couch, I lift her up into my arms to make sure she's real. Her scent fills my nostrils and I breathe her in. My Lorelei, she's real, everything about her is real. Reaching for Creed, I wrap my arm around him, holding our daughter between us.

"Thank you thank you thank you," I chant the words, until my mate's lips brush lovingly against mine silencing me.

Embracing me and Lorelei, he says. "Take me to our son."

Chapter 18
Creed

WHEN I ARRIVED WITH Lorelei, Naomi quickly filled me in on Rylie's state of mind. And after examining Lorelei she assured me the effects of the sleeping spell will wear off. Seeing my cubs nestled between me and my fated mate now, I only regret that it took longer than I expected to return to Rylie and Logan.

After I got Lorelei to safety, I couldn't just leave the three defenseless omega shifters to fend for themselves. So I reached out to the local pack for assistance. Unfortunately, the Chesterfield wolf pack isn't exactly known for their subtlety. Although I kept my distance, twenty motorcycles howling down the streets of suburbia doesn't go unnoticed. Regardless, they got the sleeping females away from the witch before the auction started. Hopefully they will be reunited with their families soon.

I still find it hard to believe it has only been a few days since I learned I'm a father to twin cubs. And I can never fully express how it feels to have finally claim my fated mate and be reunited with my entire family. However, looking upon them now with Logan sleeping snuggled next to me, and Lorelei sleeping securely in her mother's arms, it feels as if we were never apart.

Feeling nostalgic, an unbidden memory of me, Tess and Jess, waking in our parent's bed brings a smile to my face. Although my time with my father was short, the impact he had on my life is long lasting. And now that I have my own cubs, I can truly appreciate the legacy my father left me.

In a few hours my family and I will leave Westwood for Sheridan Springs. The alpha challenge awaits, and I intend to honor my parents. Now that I've defeated one monster, it's time to put an end to the last.

When Rylie awakes abruptly, I reach out to stroke my mate's hand. My heart breaks seeing fear lingering in the depths of her expressive blue eyes.

"We're all here, Goldie."

Focusing on me first, Rylie's gaze sweeps from me to Logan and finally Lorelei.

"For a moment I thought it was all a dream."

"A dream that has come true."

"I'm afraid to let her out of my sight," Rylie says, twirling her index finger around strands of Lorelei's golden locks.

"I feel that way about the three of you. I never want to be any further away from you and our cubs than I am right now."

Smiling, Rylie releases Lorelei's hair to give my hand a gentle squeeze.

"After we've had breakfast, we'll return to Sheridan Springs for the alpha challenge."

"I can't wait for Lorelei and Logan to meet my father."

"I'm sure Branson is looking forward to meeting them as well."

"I hope he can forgive me someday. I've taken so much from him. The right to defend his claim as alpha to the Sheridan Springs clan, and the opportunity to know his grandchildren," Rylie whispers as if ashamed.

"If he doesn't already, I'm sure in time your father will come to understand you didn't intentionally set out to hurt him."

"Regret and guilt lingers in my heart, nonetheless."

"You made the best decision you could for yourself and our cubs under the circumstances."

Nodding, Rylie appears unconvinced, so I ask. "Do you regret sharing your first heat with me? Do you regret keeping our cubs safe at all cost?"

"Absolutely not," she says adamantly.

"Then there's no need to harbor regret or guilt in your heart."

"Have I told you how much I love you?" She asks, intertwining our fingers.

"Not today," I lie. Truthfully, *I love you,* were the last words she whispered to me before drifting off to sleep.

"Remind me later to show you just how much I love you," she replies with a hint of mischief.

"I intend to hold you to that, Goldie."

Logan is the first to wake, and once he set his sight on his sister, his enthusiasm becomes hard to contain. Thankfully, Lorelei's eyes flutter open, putting a smile on her brother's face. Staring down at his sister, Logan's tiny hand reaches out to his sister.

"Wake up Lori," he says when Lorelei closes her eyes seconds later.

"Give her time, Moonbeam," Rylie whispers.

Hearing her mother's voice may have been the trigger Lorelei needed to wake fully. Vibrant blue eyes, that mirrors my mate's, flash open to meet mine. If the confused look on her face is an indication, I'm not what she was expecting to find when she opened her eyes.

"You're not my mommy," she says willfully,

Suddenly with just four words spoken, I know my daughter has wrapped me around her little finger.

"I'm here, Sunshine."

"Mommy," Lorelei cries, turning towards the sound of her mother's voice.

"Yes, my sunshine, it's me," Rylie says, lifting our daughter onto her lap.

From behind closed eye lids tears stream down my mate's cheeks as Logan and I watch mother and daughter embrace each other. When Rylie's eyes open all I see is the love she has for our cubs, and the love she has for me.

Smiling, she mouths. "Would you like to meet your daughter?"

"I would, very much."

"Sunshine, I have someone I'd like you to meet," Rylie says, turning Lorelei to face me once again.

"This is my daddy, Lori," Logan giggle's cheerfully climbing onto my lap. "He can be your daddy too."

Staring between me and her brother, Lorelei says. "The old lady told me my father was coming for me. Are you my father too."

Dumfounded, I nod. "Yes, I'm your father too."

Rylie's eyes meet mine and silently we agree our questions can wait. For now we'll concentrate on moving forward as a united family. The time will come soon enough, and we'll have to deal with the witch. Until then this is family time.

Chapter 19
Rylie

WHEN CALIAN OFFERED the use of his family's private jet, Creed and I thanked him for his generosity and allowed the twins a few hours of playtime with Dakota before we departed for Sheridan Springs. Logan was excited to be on a plane and in the air for the short flight, while Lorelei sat quietly between me and her father.

Entering my father's house with my fated mate and my cubs, I feel as if I've come full circle. Although I have my doubts, my father appears to have left the hurt of my betrayal in the past. According to him, his newfound status as a grandfather takes priority over his lost claim for alpha.

However, with less than twelve hours until Creed challenges the Sheridan Springs alpha, Langdon Whitmore, I'm a nervous wreck. Since my mate's challenge is one of honor, not position, and because I have no doubt that Creed will win, I don't know what will become of the Sheridan Springs clan after my mate becomes alpha. Will the Whitmores be allowed to remain a part of the clan? Will Creed stay in Sheridan Springs as its new alpha? And how will my mate becoming clan alpha impact my relationship with my father?

In celebration of our family, I help my father prepare a small feast of our favorite dishes. With my father thoroughly enchanted with his grandchildren, and Logan and Lorelei overjoyed to have a grandfather. I feel at ease leaving them in his care tomorrow while I accompany Creed to the alpha challenge.

After tucking the twins in for the night, I escort Creed to my childhood bedroom. Shutting the door, I chant a spell that will ensure our privacy. Eager to have my mate again, I practically leap into his arms.

"I think it's time I show you just how much I love you," I growl softly against his lips.

"I'm all yours," he promises seductively.

Desperate to see his body, and touch his naked flesh, I unbutton his shirt before pushing it off his shoulder onto the floor. Staring unabashedly at my mate, I take in the sight of him. Sculpted by the hands of the gods, his broad shoulders and chiseled abs are a divine thing of beauty.

Gliding my fingers down the length of Creed's muscular torso, I trace the define line of his V-cut until it disappears inside his boxer briefs. My tongue darts out to lick my lips, causing the bulge in my mate's jeans to grow larger. The sound of Creed's groan has me lifting my head up towards a set of striking twin moons. The intense fire I see twinkling in his eyes melts my core. Unable to bear the loss of skin-on-skin contact, I force myself to take a reluctant step back. Dropping to my knees, inexperienced fingers unbutton and unzip Creed's jeans. As I work to free my mate's cock, his strong reassuring hands cup my face. Fisting my hair, he gives it an eager tug urging me forward.

With Creed's cock free for the taking, I wrap both hands around the thick veiny flesh of his huge shaft. On contact my mate's cock pulses in my hands, lengthening in my grasp. Greedily, my core clenches desperately aching to be filled.

Leaning forward, I open my mouth ready to devour my mate. When needy growls fill the bedroom with the sound of hedonistic pleasure, I take Creed deeper into my mouth, hitting the back of my throat. Gliding up and down his shaft, the thought of my mate's seed sliding down my throat has me salivating with every stroke of my tongue.

"Rylie, Fuck." Creed growls. "I promised you I wouldn't waste my seed."

Remembering his promise, I want to make him break it. I want to taste him on my tongue even more. An animalistic need fuels my desire to take what I so desperately want from my fated mate. To give him the same pleasure he has given me countless times.

When Creed's heavy breathing sounds more like the growl of his bear, I know he's close to the edge. Demanding his release, I suck and stroke his cock hard and fast. My mate's promise gives way to my vow to break it when his pelvis thrusts wildly against my face chasing his release. Enviously my core clenches tightly, missing the pounding of Creed's cock.

Roaring his release, Creed's seed coats my tongue before sliding down my throat in ropes of salty goodness. Female pride spreads a smile across my lips, and I give my mate's cock a lingering suck before releasing him.

"My turn," Creed groans, lifting me into his arms.

"I'm all yours," I moan, repeating his words.

Carrying me to my bed, Creed undresses me quickly before lying me on my back. I watch with anticipation as my mate removes his own clothes. The sight of his cock and balls free from the confines of his jeans has me licking my lips once again.

And when his cock swells and lengthens before my eyes my core spasms expectantly with need.

Prowling the length of the bed, Creed rest his face between my thighs. "I can breathe in the scent of your arousal for a lifetime," he says, plunging two fingers into the depth of my needy core. "I love that you're always ready for me," he groans, sliding his fingers deeper.

My back arch reaching for the release my mate holds in the palm of his hand. He finger fucks me, quickening my breath with every thrust until I'm teetering on the brink of a much-needed orgasm. I shatter when Creed's tongue sinks into my tightening core. And I lose myself to unrestrained passion when he licks, sucks and bites my engorged bud. The pleasurable pain sends me plummeting over the edge into pure ecstasy.

Reaching for Creed, he comes willingly, covering my body with his. Effortlessly, he sinks into me filling me completely in one deep possessive thrust. Instinctively, my legs wrap tightly around Creed's waist, welcoming my mate and the beast within him. His cock claims me over and over, pounding into me in earnest until I'm screaming his name.

Sated, I lie in Creed's arms, knowing fate has given me the mate my heart needs.

• • • •

CREED AND I ENTER THE forest at sunrise ready to face the Council of Elders and the Whitmores. Although omegas aren't permitted to attend an alpha challenge, we are well aware of the fighting arena. Dubbed the Pit, the arena is no more than a large circular clearing in the forest surrounded by stones.

It's where the final two alpha candidates must prove they're worthiness to lead the clan. Knowing Langdon won four years ago when my father was forced to forfeit his right to defend his claim as alpha, I feel he may be immensely unprepared to face my mate, a true alpha.

Calling the challenge to order, Preema gains everyone's attention. All seven-council members are present, although only three are required to attend an alpha challenge. Beau stands next to his son, sneering in Creed's direction.

"Before we officially begin we must go over the rules of the alpha challenge," Preema announces.

"Our rules don't apply to a non-clan member," Langdon is quick to point out.

"Which is why we need to establish a few rules both parties can agree on," Preema retorts.

"I only need to know if we fight in our human skin or our bear's?" Creed asks.

"Bear," Beau says, and Langdon agrees.

"I assume you have no objections?" Langdon questions.

"None whatsoever," Creed declares.

"Very well. You will fight fully shifted until one of you yields," Preema surmises.

"Until the death," Langdon challenges. "And once I've solidified my claim as alpha, the omega will sever her mate bond with the outsider and return to the Sheridan Springs clan as a breeder."

Unable to hold back my anger, I growl menacingly. "I'd die before I give in to you or your outdated breeding laws."

"You will submit, omega," Langdon snaps, stepping to me.

Taking me by the hand, Creed positions himself between me and Langdon.

"Come any closer, and your father will see how quickly you die before his eyes." Creed roars ominously.

Interrupting the standoff, Preema directs Creed and Langdon to the Pit. At six feet five inches tall, Creed towers over most males, and his bear is no different. My mate's Kodiak stands at least three feet taller. Stepping into the Pit, they wait for the challenge to officially start before shifting into their bears.

"Shift!" Preema shouts, stepping out of the Pit.

Langdon shifts first as Creed watches him. Having never seen Langdon's grizzly, I'm surprised when his bear isn't much taller than mine. Still in his human form, Creed charges the bear, knocking him to the ground. Langdon's bear scrambles to his feet. Positioning himself at the animal's back, Creed puts the beast in a chokehold. Unable to look away, I watch the flex of Creed's muscles tighten around the neck of Langdon's bear. Struggling to remain standing, the bear drops to one knee and then the other before managing to roll onto his back pinning Creed beneath him.

Breaking his hold on the bear, Creed shoves it forward, freeing himself. Langdon's bear gets to his feet first and begins swiping wildly at Creed. When his claw tears down Creed's torso, my heart stalls momentarily at the sight of my mate's blood falling to the forest floor.

I can only assume Langdon feels victorious after drawing first blood when he advanced towards Creed ready to strike another blow. Grabbing the bear by his extended paw, Creed manages to hip toss the beast. Landing with a thud, Langdon's bear roars startling the animals of the forest.

Suddenly it occurs to me that Creed is intentionally baiting the Whitmores. Thirty years ago, Beau challenged Creed's father, Daniel. However, when Beau lost the challenge to Creed's father, who had won in his human form, a jealous and vindictive Beau shifted and attacked Daniel from behind, mauling him to death in front of his fated mate and son. I can understand why Creed fights Langdon's bear in his human form. Defeating Langdon this way will honor both his parents. Personally, I'm looking forward to the Whitmores downfall.

Turning my attention back to the Pit, I somehow missed what caused Langdon's bear paw to bleed. Until I notice two bloody black claws in my mate's grip. Unable to contain my amusement. I chuckle loudly, earning me a chastising look of disapproval from a few council members.

Not giving a single fuck if it's permitted or not, I cheer for my mate, but not long enough to be a distraction to him. Unfortunately, the same can't be said for Langdon. I panic when I see the sinister black eyes of his bear racing toward me. Council members scatter quickly leaving me alone in the path of an angry grizzly. I scramble to get away, but I'm too late when the large bear charges me. Lying on my back, I fear what Langdon's bear would do next. My fears are quickly dashed when my mate tackles the bear to the ground. Creed's claws extend, ready to rip the bear apart.

"Yield or I'll rip your fucking heart out," Creed growls.

Shifting back to his human form, Langdon yields, relinquishing the role of clan alpha to Creed. Both men get to their feet, as Preema enters the Pit. Turning to face the council, Preema proclaims Creed, Sheridan Springs new clan alpha. Interrupting, Beau declares the challenge invalid.

Addressing the Council of Elders, Preema asks. "Shall we put the final decision to a vote."

"Your ruling stands, Madame Council," Denna says, after conferring with the others.

A rejected Langdon attempts to shift, until Creed's massive paw wraps around his throat.

"Just like your father," Creed accuses. "You Whitmores never seem to know when you've lost. Shall I keep my promise and let your father see how quickly you die?"

Gasping for air, Langdon's face takes on a sickly hue before his father's eyes.

"Don't kill him!" Beau shouts. "He's your brother."

Shocked by Beau's claim, Creed's hold on Langdon's throat falls away. My mate stares unbelievingly at the male who murdered his father and raped his mother.

"I scented your mother's heat the day I killed your father," Beau confesses.

Without warning Creed swipes Langdon's bare chest, and Beau whimpers. Scenting Langdon's fresh blood, I watch my mate, shatter beneath the weight of Beau's confession.

Assuming Creed recognizes his kin. Beau continues. "After Willa gave birth to my cub she ran away. And since she'd given me a son, I didn't go after her."

"Don't you fucking dare speak my mother's name," Creed warns.

"If your brother's blood doesn't convince you of the truth, ask Preema, she knew your mother."

Creed and I turn to face Preema, and the guilt marring her features is there for all to see.

"It was my responsibility to care for the omegas when it was time for them to give birth. But Willa and I had always been friends. I was genuinely happy for her when she found her fated mate. And it broke my heart when she returned to Sheridan Springs with Beau. I witnessed her dying a little every day being away from her cubs. So when Beau finally got what he wanted I helped her escape."

"So she ran back to Timber Valley and left my newborn cub without his mother?"

"You've got to be kidding me. You killed her fated mate, forced her to leave her cubs, you sexually abused her, but you have the audacity to feel slighted because she left you with a cub she never wanted with you," Preema rants furiously.

"Did my mother leave my brother behind?" Creed asks, and I can hear the pain of his own abandonment in his tone.

"No, she didn't. The cub your mother gave birth to, a female, died."

"You're a liar, my son stands here before us," Beau fumes.

"I've been holding onto this secret for thirty years," Preema confesses. "Now I think it's time you all knew the truth."

"And what truth is that?" Creed asks.

"Your mother wasn't the only female Beau bedded during her time here. She was just the only omega. And he needed an omega to be considered for the alpha challenge. Unfortunately for Beau he lost his chance at becoming alpha when the omega he was promised found her fated mate. Which meant he couldn't challenge Branson, whose father was alpha before him."

"So he challenged my father, the Timber Valley alpha instead, to reclaim my mother, Creed clarifies.

"Precisely." Preema confirms. "Because we were friends before she left Sheridan Springs, she confided in me when Beau forced her to return. She told me her fated mate had died during the challenge, and she left her cubs in Timber Valley to keep them safe. Now I know Daniel was killed in a cowardly fashion by Beau."

Beau sneers hearing Preema's assessment of his actions. Ignoring him Preema continues.

"When Willa became pregnant with Beau's cub, she begged me to help her end the pregnancy. I refused and she ended our friendship. We didn't speak again until the night she went into labor. After hours of labor, she pushed the cub out. It breathed for a few minutes before its heart stop. Willa had lost a lot of blood and was too weak to stay awake. While Willa slept, Ana, a beta, gave birth to a healthy cub, a son."

"Langdon." I provide.

"Both females had given birth to cubs fathered by Beau. But only one survived. Since Ana never wanted to have cubs, she went along with my plan to save Willa. We knew if she stayed Beau would only try to impregnate her again. When Willa woke, we told her the truth, that her cub died. Ana told Willa she would let Beau believe her son is Willa's after we helped her escape. We knew that if Beau believed his son was born of an omega, his son could become alpha someday even if he couldn't."

"I would know if my son's mother was a beta," Beau snaps.

"Have you ever taken the time to scent his blood," Creed ask, smelling Langdon's blood on his finger.

"Of course, I know my son's bloodline."

"I do smell the blood of my kin," Creed says, "But there isn't a hint of my mother's omega blood."

"Ana was your mother's cousin. So that makes her your kin."

"And so is Langdon," I add.

Nodding, Preema turns to face Langdon who has remained quiet throughout the revelation. "I'm sorry to inform you, but you have no true claim as alpha."

"Do you think I'm going to allow some outsider to take away my birthright?" Langdon growls.

"Creed didn't take it away; it was never truly yours to claim. Your mother, Ana, a beta, gave you the opportunity to be better than your station, better than your father, but you chose to follow in his footsteps."

"This is all your fault, you useless fucking omega."

Stepping to me Langdon's words are meant to hurt and degrade me, but they have no effect whatsoever. I know my worth. Unfortunately for him, Creed has a different opinion on the matter. Landing a blow to Langdon's nose, my mate knocks him on his bare ass.

"Some people never learn," I chastise. And because I'm in the mood to assert a little power of my own. I chant a spell to cover Langdon's private parts. "I'm sure we're all tired of seeing your dangly bits."

"What the fuck!" Langdon exclaims.

"No one from the Sheridan Springs clan has ever been able to wield magic. What makes this omega special?" Beau questions.

"Our clan hasn't had a true alpha for three generations, and now we have an omega capable of wielding magic." Preema says. "Can't you all see how the gods are blessing us."

The forest remains silent for long seconds as if it were bowing down to a true alpha, my fated mate.

"Since all the members of the Council of Elders are present, I should let you know, as Sheridan Springs new alpha, I intend to abolish the omega breeding law permanently."

Nodding, Preema and Denna are the first to agree. Until one by one all members, except Beau, accepts Creed's ruling.

"The omega breeding laws, and the alpha challenges are the foundations of this clan. You can't simply change the way we do things on a whim," Beau gripes.

"I can and I will," Creed says adamantly. "However, my first order of business as alpha should have been getting rid of the riff raff."

"What the fuck is that supposed to mean?" Langdon asks.

"What it means, cousin," Creed says mockingly. "From this day forward, Beauregard Whitmore, Langdon Whitmore, as the true alpha to the Sheridan Springs clan, I Creed Masterson, abjure you both from this day until your last. You are forever banished from the Sheridan Springs clan."

Beau growls painfully as the bond that tethers him to the clan falls away. Moments later, Langdon's pain is just as palpable.

"Leave the Sheridan Springs territory before the sunsets," Creed demands.

The clanless bear shifters look to the Council of Elders for help, only to be met with silence and the sight of their backs.

"We're done here," Creed says, effectively dismissing the six remaining council members.

Left alone in the forest, my mate takes me by the hand, leading me away from the Pit. With so many unanswered questions still lingering in my mind, Creed and I need to find the time to discuss our future. Now that he's alpha to two territories, I wonder what's next for us.

Chapter 20
Creed

ALTHOUGH I INTENDED to kill both Whitmores, I'm satisfied that the outcome honors my parents and my fated mate. Now that I'm apparently alpha to two packs, Rylie and I have some decisions to make soon. Hopefully a return to our normal routines will provide us with some answers.

However, for now all that can wait. Tonight I intend to read my cubs a bedtime story. Peeking into the guest bedroom of my cubs' grandfather's home, two sets of inquisitive eyes greets me. Logan's gray eyes, beams with excitement ready to be tucked in. Unfortunately, the shine of Lorelei's blue gaze leaves her eyes when she sees me. No doubt she was expecting her mother. Undeterred, I enter the bedroom, ready to win my daughter over, one bedtime story at a time.

"Who's ready for a bedtime story," I ask.

"Me," Logan squeals happily.

"What about you, Angel? Would you like to hear a bedtime story?"

Nodding, she says. "No scarry stories."

My heartbreaks, imagining what haunts my little angel's dreams.

"I promise. I got this book especially for you and your brother."

Pulling the small hardcover book from a plastic bag, I show it to my cubs. Lorelei is the first to react, hiding her head under the bedcover. Logan is more vocal, coming to his sister's rescue.

"The bear is a monster; he hurt mommy and took Lori."

Understanding Lorelei's distress, I put the book away. Although my cubs are nearly four years old, I'm still getting to know them both. I'm learning that Logan is fiercely protective of Lorelei, and she has intellect far beyond her years. Starting from the beginning, I share a story from my heart.

"Did the daddy go home to his family?" Lorelei whispers when the story ends.

"He did, and when he found his family he was the happiest person in the world."

"You found us, daddy," Logan says.

"And being your father makes me the happiest father in the world."

Pushing away the bedcover, Logan crawls out of bed. I welcome the little arms that wrap around my neck. Giving me a hug, he says. "I'm glad you're my daddy."

"Thank you, Logan. I'm so glad you're my son."

Desperate to connect with my daughter, I extend a hand to Lorelei. Hesitantly, she reach for me, but withdraws her hand at the last second. Deciding it's time for the twins to get some sleep, I carry Logan back to bed. After tucking him in, I place a kiss on his forehead.

"Good night, son."

"Good night, daddy."

Making my way to Lorelei's side of the bed, I tuck her in as well. However, instead of kissing her forehead, I offer her a smile, and simply say good night. I'm at the door ready to leave the bedroom when her sleepy voice calls out to me.

"Daddy."

Standing motionless at the door, I wait hopefully for my daughter's next words. I knew in that moment it didn't matter how long it took, I would wait.

"You didn't kiss my forehead," she whispers shyly.

Returning to Lorelei's side of the bed, I kneel to kiss my little angel's forehead.

"Will you keep the monster away?"

For a moment I forget my daughter's boundaries, and I lift her up into my arms. When she doesn't push me away, I cradle her against my heart, promising to keep the monster away, promising to always protect her.

After a few minutes the room fills with the blissful sound of my daughter sleeping peacefully in my arms. Tucking Lorelei back under the covers, I give her a kiss on each of her cherub cheeks.

• • • •

STEPPING OUT ONTO THE back porch, I find my mate and her father enjoying the night air. With both of them here, I can only assume fate is telling me to seize the moment. I clear my throat, effectively gaining there attention.

Smiling, my mate asks. "Did they give you a hard time?"

Still blown away by my cubs, I reply with extreme bias. "They're perfect."

Nodding, Branson agrees, but Rylie shakes her head as if she knows better.

"I need to speak with you both," I say, moving pass the topic of my cubs. "I'd like to share my thoughts with you about how we move forward as a family and a clan."

"What's on your mind, son?" Branson asks.

Hearing the fatherly concern in Branson's voice reminds me of my own father, it also reminds me how much I enjoy being called *son*.

"I was thinking of merging the Timber Valley and Sheridan Springs clans."

"You're alpha to both clans, so it only makes sense to bring them together," Branson says.

"Where will we live?" Rylie asks. "Westwood is the only home Logan and Lorelei has known since they were born. And we have people there that truly care about us. I don't want to just walk away from them."

"You don't have to, at least not right away. For the next five years we'll call Westwood home until my contract with the sheriff's office ends. Does that work for you?"

Leaping into my arms, Rylie says. "That works for us."

"Now that we've settled where we'll live for the next five years. Branson I need your help here in Sheridan Springs."

"Whatever I can do to help, I'm glad to do it as long as you keep that smile on my daughter's face."

"I hope you still feel that way when you hear what I'm asking."

"What is it, son?"

"I can't be in three places at once, so I'll need someone I trust, someone who has my family's best interest at heart. I need an alpha with a proven track record to lead the clan in my absence."

"I'm no longer an alpha," Branson corrects.

"That's not what I've learned from my mate. Your father was alpha before you and his father before him. And if you had a son, the line of alpha's from the Adams bloodline would have continued."

"And someday your grandson will become alpha," Rylie adds.

"Contests don't create alphas; true alphas are born from the bloodline of a true alpha."

"In that case, I'd be honor to lead the clan for as long as you ask it of me."

"Timber Valley is where my mate and our cubs will call home someday." Seeking Rylie's reaction, I continue when she gives me an approving nod. "And someday my son will choose his own home. Until then I know his grandfather will protect his birthright."

A shift in the air alerts my mate, Branson and myself, to an intruder entering the back yard. Turning to face the disturbance, I wish I could say I'm surprised to see Beau Whitmore walking out of the shadows. Placing myself between the unwelcomed visitor and my mate, I issue a warning.

"You should leave while you still can, Whitmore."

"I was on my way out of town when I understood how this had to end," Whitmore says, disregarding my warning. "There's no way I can walk away knowing you have it all. Like your father you have taken everything from me. So either I kill you or you kill me, Masterson."

Leaping off the porch, the challenge was over before it began. I knew if I spared him again he would return again and again for my mate, or my cubs. Choosing to end his life quickly, I snapped his neck before he was able to shift. With Beau's lifeless body lying at my feet, I peer into the darkness finding the hate filled black eyes of his son staring back at me. Lowering his head submissively, Langdon slowly retreats.

"I'll take care of this," Branson says, hefting the body onto his shoulder.

Nodding, I silently offer my thanks. I don't know how long I stood in the back yard after Branson left, listening to the sounds of the night. Listening for anything that my pose a threat to my fated mate or our cubs. When I'm satisfied all is as it should be, I lift Rylie up into my arms and carry her upstairs to our bed.

Behind the closed door of the spelled walls of Rylie's childhood bedroom, the only sound I want to hear is my mate calling my name.

• • • •

AFTER ADDRESSING THE Council of Elders, early Sunday morning, I formally reinstate my mate's father as alpha to the Sheridan Springs clan. And by 10:00 a.m. Branson, Rylie, our cubs and I are on the road heading to Timber Valley. Branson accompanying us serves a dual purpose, I would like him to be there when I inform my uncle Franklin I'm merging the clans. As the current alpha to the Timber Valley clan, Frank will continue to lead the clan for the next five years. Branson also has a role to play, which is the real reason I asked him to join us on this trip.

With the help of my sisters, Jess and Tess, I'm planning a surprise for Rylie. Although she once refer to it as marriage, it's much more than that. Our bonding ceremony will connect my fated mate and I on a level that infinitely surpasses a human wedding.

When we arrive at my family's homestead, Jess and Tess are there to greet us. Unlike my arrival four days ago, they don't come running to me, they make a beeline to Rylie and our cubs. I quickly introduce Branson before my sisters get wrapped up in welcoming my mate and our cubs. They give Branson an identical smile and a rushed hello, before opening the back passenger door of his pickup. Jess greets Rylie with a hug, before stepping aside to allow her to climb out. Tess greets Rylie equally cheerfully, before turning her attention to our cubs.

"You must be Lorelei and Logan, I'm your auntie Tess, and this is my twin sister Jess."

Taking Lorelei by the hand, Logan says. "Lori is my twin sister."

"I know, little one. Would you like to meet your cousins?" Tess asks, pointing towards the house.

From the front porch, Wade holds the hand of two of his four daughters. Stepping off the porch my sister's mate brings their cubs closer.

"Their little," Logan pouts. "And girls."

Laughing, Jess says. "If you don't want to play with the little girls, maybe you can help me with the horses."

Logan turns his attention to Jess, nodding when she offers to help him climb out of the vehicle. Releasing Lorelei's hand he looks to me and his mother for approval.

"Have fun, and listen to your auntie Jess," Rylie says, granting Logan permission to leave with my sister.

"How about you, Lorelei? Would you like to meet your cousins?" Tess asks.

"Can we have a tea party?"

"Absolutely, we love tea parties."

Climbing out of the vehicle with Tess's help, Lorelei reaches for her mother once her little feet hit the ground.

"I'll see you later," Rylie says, pushing up her tiptoes to reach my lips.

A much too short tender kiss later she's being ushered into the house for a tea party. Left alone with Branson, we make our way to the lake for a casual meeting with Franklin. An afternoon of fishing with my uncle and my mate's father will be a bonding ceremony of sorts. It's important the alphas of both my clans are on the same page moving forward. While Branson, reign as alpha ends when my son comes of age, Franklin's role as alpha to Timber Valley will end in five years when I return home permanently.

Although my uncle never wanted to be alpha, I have to admit he's done one helluva job leading the clan. He's the reason I was never forced to lead our clan even when I became old enough to do so. He allowed me the time I needed to find my way back to claiming my birthright.

Arriving at the lake, my uncle greets Branson and I with a cold beer. Eager to get clan business out of the way first, I bring Frank up to speed with all that's happened in Sheridan Springs. Expectantly, my uncle is pleased to hear his time as alpha is coming to an end. Thirty years is a long time to dedicate yourself to a job you never wanted. When his mate died giving birth to his son Kurt, it almost destroyed him. Unlike my mother, Franklin found a way to stay strong despite losing his fated mate. He lived for Kurt, my sisters and I, and our clan.

The sun is setting when Franklin, Branson and I return to the main house without a single fish among us. Luckily, my sisters have prepared a feast in honor of the bonding ceremony. Now all I have to do is get my fated mate to the ceremonial site.

Entering my bedroom, Rylie greets me wearing my mother's ceremonial gown. The flowing white gown has been in my mother's family for generations. Tess was the last to wear it three years ago.

"Jess didn't want me to be blindsided when you escorted me to the ceremonial site. She said I have the right to prepare for such an important moment in our lives."

Seeing the joy in Rylie's eyes, for once I'm happy my sister's inability to keep a secret hasn't altered my plans.

"You're absolutely beautiful, Goldie."

Blushing, she says, "And you smell absolutely horrible."

Giving her a deep lingering kiss, I'm careful not to ruin the dress. Her moans harden my cock and I force myself to step away before we get carried away.

"It's not me, it's the fish," I say, tugging my sweaty T-shirt over my head.

"Either way, you need to shower and change, we have a date to keep."

"Yes, Ma'am," I salute.

Knowing I've won the heart of this astonishing female, grateful the gods have found me worthy of such an exceptional creature, I welcome what fate has in store for us.

• • • •

Epilogue
Rylie

AFTER OUR BONDING CEREMONY, Creed and I spent a few nights alone in the cabin. Starting our life together where it all began seems fated to me. My mate and I have made a lot of decisions about the life we want together. Inherently, omegas are born to breed, but that doesn't mean we have to be ruled by our heat and pop out cubs every six months. Creed and I want more cubs, just not right now. We want to give Logan and Lorelei time to get used to having both parents and an extended family.

My father returned to Sheridan Springs the day after the bonding ceremony, with Kurt in tow. According to my mate's cousin, his fated mate has to be in Sheridan Springs, because he hasn't found her in Timber Valley.

Creed, Logan, Lorelei and I have been back in Westwood two weeks now. Although we're still in transition, so to speak, getting back to our normal routines has helped. I'm back at the hospital working part-time now that Symone has left suddenly for New Orleans. The twins and I will miss her, but I can't complain when my new roommate is my fated mate. It took me some time to convince Creed, renting Naomi's cottage is our best option. The grounds are protected which means the twins are safer here than at Westwood Inn. However, we did agree to move our cubs upstairs to the loft bedroom. I know we'll outgrow the cottage before Creed's contract with the sheriff's office ends, until then this is our home.

Tonight the twins are out of the house, Logan has a sleepover with Dakota, and Lorelei has girls night with Naomi. Which means despite the privacy spell in place when we're alone in our bedroom, my mate and I need to connect on a deeper level. With our cubs out of the house we can shift in the forest and allow our bears to roam free. Creed has promised to take me to his bear's den. Knowing my mate always keeps his promises I'm looking forward to our night together more than ever.

Anticipating the arrival of my fated mate, has me brimming with excitement. Our bears haven't been together since our bonding ceremony, quite frankly my grizzly misses her Kodiak. The sound of Creed's footsteps approaching, and the scent of him in the air tightens my core expectantly. I wait for my mate patiently despite an untamable need to run to him and my bear's mental urging.

Moments later, I'm rewarded for my patience, when Creed enters the cottage, All six foot five inches of him topped with a Stetson that makes him sinfully sexy and hard to resist. Needing to breathe him in, I step into his waiting arms.

"I've missed you," I moan against his broad chest.

Removing his Stetson, he says. "I didn't mean to keep you waiting, my heart."

I blush like a giddy schoolgirl every time he calls me, *my heart*. With Creed it has always been about claiming my heart, and when he claims my heat, I know it's because he truly loves me.

"I got a call from Kurt today," Creed says cheerfully.

Lifting my head to give him my full attention, I ask. "Is he okay?"

"He's more than okay." Creed assures me as he leads me to the couch. "Turns out he was right. He did find his fated mate among the Sheridan Springs clan."

"Who's the female," I ask curiously.

"Kurt has found his fated mate in Denna."

"You're kidding!"

"Not at all. He said their meeting triggered Denna's heat, and they knew instantly.

"Denna has never..."

"I know, she thought she was barren because of a childhood accident. Not so since her mate has impregnated her."

"Do you think this has anything to do with you merging the clan or our true alpha-omega bond?"

"It's possible I suppose, or fate was just waiting for the right time for them to meet their destiny."

Climbing onto Creed's lap, I whisper. "It's time you kept your promise."

Eagerly, Creed stands, and purposeful strides carry me out the back door. The sound of nature welcomes us as a full moon glistens in the night sky of the forest. Entering the den of Creed's bear, I take in the surroundings of the cave. Although it's clear the space is meant for a bear, the cozy nook with a bedroll is obviously intended for our human half.

'This is great."

"I'm glad you like it."

Teasingly, I take a step away from Creed, removing my clothes, I let them fall at my feet onto the cave floor. Baring my body and soul to my mate, I chant a spell to remove his clothes.

Smirking, Creed says. "I wanted to give you a show, my heart."

Needing to feel the warmth of Creed's flesh against mine, I lead him to the bedroll. On my hands and knees, I invite my mate to take me from behind. Bending over me, the tight embrace of Creed's arms wrap around my torso as he pulls me onto his lap. I'm unprepared when his enormous cock slams into me, filling me utterly. I'm unprepared when my orgasm shatters me completely. Allowing animalistic mating instincts to takeover, I growl my release into the night. My core clenches greedily around Creed's cock, begging for more.

Seeking the passion of Creed's lips, I offer him my mouth. His tongue plunges into my mouth possessively. Lips, teeth and tongue, assault my mouth with the heat of kisses I never want to end. Our moans of pleasure mingles in the air, causing my core to spasm in sync with our erotic sounds. With Creed's cock buried deep inside me he gives me everything I'll ever want or need when his seed fills me.

Lying sated in the protective embrace of my fated mate, I thank the gods for blessing me with Creed, a true alpha to claim the heart of this omega.

• • • •

Thank You

I WANT TO THANK YOU for reading Heart of the Omega, book two in the Fated Mates of Westwood series. I hope you enjoy getting to know Rylie Adams and her fated mate, Creed Masterson, as much as I have.

If you haven't done so already, please take the time to review my book. It's the best way for readers to find lesser-known authors. And if you have, thank you so much, I truly appreciate your support.

I would also like to thank MiblArt for the cover design. You rock!

• • • •

Happy Reading and Happy Endings!

About the Author

Reese Spenser is both author and a ravenous reader of romance. She began her career as a contemporary romance author with her debut novel Tainted Bond. However, she has always been fascinated with the supernatural. It was her weakness for vampires and shifters, and her addiction to mythology and fairytales, that led her to begin writing paranormal romance. When she's not busy writing, she enjoys spending time with family and friends and spoiling her grandchildren.

Read more at reesespenser.com.

Milton Keynes UK
Ingram Content Group UK Ltd.
UKHW011254221123
433051UK00006B/311